ALL HOPE IS LOST

ALL HOPE IS LOST

BY
MATTHEW GENE

Progressive
RISING PHOENIX PRESS ®

Published 2025
by Progressive Rising Phoenix Press, LLC
www.progressiverisingphoenix.com

ISBN: 978-1-958640-80-7

Printed in the U.S.A.
1st Printing

Cover image by Christophe Kiciak, Copyright: 2025, Used
with Permission.

Snake Illustrations by Matthew Gene, Copyright: 2025, Used
with Permission.

Title Page Illustration: "Black and White Vector Silhouette of
Kneeling Fallen Angel with Large Wings," by Woman from
Baku. ShutterStock ID: 2570651203, used under license from
ShutterStock.com.

Chapter Heading Illustration: "Angel Wing Illustration Vector,
Wings Graphic Element," by gfx_nazim. ShutterStock ID:
2410531721, used under license from ShutterStock.com.

Book and Cover design by William Speir
Visit: http://www.williamspeir.com

All the world is made of faith, and trust, and pixie dust.

- J.M. Barrie, Peter Pan

There are other worlds than these.

- Jake Chambers
The Gunslinger by Stephen King

Book 1

DUPLICITY

1

The sound of machinery hammered through his skull, relentless and metallic. Each strike shook something deep inside, like it was pounding on bone instead of air. The noise wouldn't stop. He tried to open his eyes, but they wouldn't cooperate; they felt glued shut, heavy, as if someone had pressed weights on his lids. His wrists burned where cold metal bit into his skin. Every time he moved, the chains snapped tight and dragged at his arms until pain crawled up his shoulders. The headache, maybe a concussion, could explain the pounding. But not the hissing.

Something else was there, breathing and alive.

He heard the scrape of claws across stone before feeling them slice into his arm. Panic took over, forcing his eyes open just enough to see. A shape shifted in the dark, slick and black, its surface sliding like oil on water. The thing gleamed faintly, as though it was lit from somewhere deep inside itself. It wouldn't stay still. Its body broke apart and reformed in slow, liquid movements that almost seemed deliberate. Then those eyes appeared, bright green, and unblinking. Below them, a grin full of teeth spread too wide to belong to anything human. Fingers, or something close to them, reached toward him, long and sharp.

He jerked back against the slab, but the chains held. The dark surged again, and he passed out.

When he woke, there was warmth. Not the kind that burns, but a deeper, steady heat that seemed to hold him. Smoke hung in the air, glowing orange as it moved. He blinked until shapes formed; then he saw fire. It licked across a pair of wings, white in form, but alive with light. The flames didn't consume them; they *belonged* to them. And the wings belonged to a massive figure that stood certain, while the ground trembled with each step it took. In its hands, a sword blazed like the wings, fire living on it, pulsing and breathing as if it shared one heart with the creature that held it.

The figure lifted the sword high, pointing it toward the sky, then turned the blade in one smooth motion towards the ground. It lowered its gaze, with eyes the color of molten glass, red and yellow swirling, locked onto him.

A single word cut through the air.

3

Remember.

The blade fell, with both hands driving it into stone. The world split open, lightning flared, white and violent, and the thunder that followed an instant later, violent, swallowing everything.

2

Christopher jolted upright in bed with his heart pounding and his body drenched in cold sweat. The loud bang outside his window had yanked him from a nightmare, leaving his chest heaving with each breath.

BAM!

He flinched again; the noise pulled him back to reality. The clock on his nightstand read 11 a.m. He groaned. He'd slept in late, later than he meant to. And the weight of too much sleep clung to him.

Outside the window, his friend Tommy and Mr. Price were working on the old, stubborn Ford truck. The backfiring engine had startled him, leaving him with a feeling of relief and lingering unease.

He rubbed his eyes and let out a shaky breath. Most of the dream was already slipping away, yet two things stayed sharp in his mind: the green eyes glowing in the dark, and the voice that spoke that single word.

Remember.

The word echoed in him like it had been branded there. He shook his head, tried to drive it away, but it refused to fade. It had not felt like any dream he had ever had. It felt forced, as though something had pressed itself into his mind.

He pushed the blanket aside and swung his legs over the bed. Tommy and Mr. Price were still bent under the hood of the Ford, Tommy's laugh carrying faintly through the glass. The sound grounded him, but he still needed air.

Christopher stood and made his way toward the shower, hoping the hot water and steam might burn the memory from his mind. But as he moved, he felt that no matter what he did, he wouldn't be able to shake it. The dream would follow him the way fear sometimes does. And once he saw Tommy, he would have to decide how much of it to share.

3

The Ford pickup roared to life with a loud rattling noise, and smoke billowed from the tailpipe. Mr. Price sat behind the wheel, gripping it tight with determination, his knuckles turning white. He was intent on keeping the engine running.

Tommy stood outside the truck, watching his father with a mix of admiration and exasperation. *What would it take for you to give up on this truck?* he wondered. But he already knew the answer. Mr. Price never gave up on anything. He'd rather get the truck running just to prove a point, and if it still gave him trouble, he'd destroy it himself to assert his control. Mr. Price had a deep disdain for modern gadgets and conveniences that promised to improve life but ended up frustratingly complicated or cheaply made.

Within thirty seconds, the truck sputtered, coughed, and died with one final bang from the tailpipe.

BAM!

"Ah, damn it!" Mr. Price yelled, slapping the steering wheel in frustration.

Hearing the commotion, Christopher appeared behind Tommy with a grin on his face. "I heard you were working on the truck."

Mr. Price looked up from behind the steering wheel and eyed Christopher with a mock glare. "Tommy, tell your friend over there that if he doesn't watch his mouth, I'll have him under the hood helping us figure out what's wrong with it."

"How long you been standing there?" Tommy asked, glanced over his shoulder.

"Oh, around 'damn it.'"

Tommy laughed. "So, what are you gonna do today?"

"Oh, I don't know. I hoped you'd have some ideas."

"Well, the least you two can do is help me push this damn thing back to the side of the house," Mr. Price said, gesturing towards the back of the truck with a single thumb.

"What do you think? Should we help him?" Tommy asked.

"Sure, why not? My old man is your old man, right?"

The boys moved to the rear of the truck while Mr.

Price steered it into place. Together, they got the Ford back to its familiar resting spot at the side of the house.

"My old man is your old man."

Tommy had said that a couple of summers back, during a rough patch in Christopher's life. He had grown up without a father, leaving his mother to raise him alone. She tried her best, but some things couldn't be filled. In small ways, Mr. Price stepped into that gap. Even now, standing in the cold with grease on his jacket, he carried a steadiness Christopher secretly wished he could claim as his own.

The boys headed to Tommy's room. Christopher liked Tommy's room, actually, he liked the whole house, saying he enjoyed the laid-back atmosphere. Tommy was the kind of guy who didn't play sports in high school but still had plenty of friends.

"So, what do you wanna do?" Tommy asked.

"I'm not sure. Actually, I wanted to talk to you about something."

"Oh great, you're not turned weird on me, are you?" Tommy teased, raising an eyebrow.

"Ha! Stop! I want to tell you about a dream I had."

"Not another dream about the girls' volleyball team, is it?"

"No. Are you done now?" Christopher asked.

"Yeah, okay, I'm listening. What's up?"

Christopher leaned forward, his tone shifted to something more serious. "I don't remember all of it, but I do remember these green eyes looking at me. The kind you don't forget. And then an angel, on fire, holding a sword. It struck the sword against the ground. But right before it did that, the angel said one word."

Tommy frowned. "Man, that sounds like some kind of horror movie. You sure you didn't fall asleep with the TV on?"

Christopher shook his head. "No. It felt… different. It wasn't like a regular dream. It felt pushed into me."

"And the angel? What did it say?"

"Remember," Christopher said.

"Remember what?" Tommy inquired, leaning back, while studying him.

Christopher didn't respond, staring into nowhere, struggling to recall.

"So… what do you think it means?"

"I don't know," Christopher admitted. "I've got a bad feeling about this, like it wasn't just a dream." He dropped onto the bed, stared down at his feet, feeling drained.

Tommy watched him, puzzled by his friend's behavior. It wasn't like Christopher to get worked up over something like this. Normally, he was pretty calm and cool about everything, and always up for cruising around in his mother's Oldsmobile, which he was allowed to use during school hours and on weekends. Something was definitely bothering him, but Tommy decided not to press the issue just yet. He'd wait until Christopher was ready to talk. Still, a chill ran down his spine the way he had said it. The words carried weight, heavier than just a bad dream.

Two quick knocks sounded at the door.

"That's probably my dad. Hold on," Tommy said.

As the door opened, Mr. Price stood there. He pulled a peach away from his mouth, and shifted the big chunk he'd just bit over to one side so he could speak. "Hey, boys. Whatcha up to?"

"Oh, just…" Tommy began.

"Shootin' the breeze?" Mr. Price finished.

"Well, I guess you could say that."

Christopher looked at Mr. Price. "What are you eatin' there, David?"

Mr. Price straightened up. He didn't mind if Christopher called him David, he was the only one who could get away with it, not even Tommy.

"Well, if you must know, Chris, I'm eating a Weatherford peach straight from Weatherford, Texas."

Christopher smirked, not impressed.

"Why, it's the best damn peach in the world," David declared.

Christopher grinned and looked at Tommy for help.

"So, what's up, Dad?" Tommy asked.

"Your mom and I are about to have lunch. You boys wanna join us?"

"You feel like eating?" Tommy asked Christopher.

"I am hungry. That sounds pretty good. Sure."

"Ok. Let's eat!" Mr. Price spun on his heels and headed back to the kitchen.

Christopher stood, and the dream pressed against him again. Not all of it, most of the images had slipped away, but the angel's voice still echoed.

Remember.

He forced the memory aside, not wanting Tommy or Mr. Price to notice the unease in his face.

4

The savory scent of ham with mustard sauce filled the air as Christopher stepped into the kitchen. The warmth and coziness of the Price household embraced him, stirring an ache of longing for a sense of home that felt this close-knit. His eyes found Katherine Price, her figure blurred by the steam rising from a large pan on the stove, and a smile spread across her face as she noticed him.

"Well, hello, Chris! You caught me with my head in the ham. Are you hungry?" Katherine's voice was warm and inviting, a reflection of the comfort he often found in this home.

"Yes, ma'am!" he responded eagerly, the anticipation of a home-cooked meal lifting his spirits.

"Then grab yourself a chair, sit down, and get ready," she encouraged, her enthusiasm contagious.

"You better listen to her, Chris. She's got that look in her eye," David added, taking another bite of the peach he had been savoring.

"David! You get that peach out of your mouth right now. I didn't spend all morning sweating in this kitchen just to watch you eat half a plate of food," she scolded playfully, her tone light yet firm.

Christopher and Tommy exchanged amused glances as David froze mid-chew, reluctantly swallowing the last bite before dropping the remainder into the trash can behind his chair.

Katherine's demeanor softened as she turned back to Christopher. "Do you like green peas, Chris?"

"Yes, ma'am." He couldn't help but laugh on the inside after witnessing David's reprimand.

She placed a plate in front of him, piled high with two slices of ham drizzled in mustard sauce, a generous helping of peas, mashed potatoes, and two fluffy biscuits. "What do you think of that?" she asked, her eyes twinkling with satisfaction.

"Mrs. Price, I don't know if I'm going to be able to eat all this," he admitted, eyeing the plate with a mix of awe and nervousness.

"Would you stop calling me Mrs. Price? You've known me long enough to call me Katherine, or even Mom, if you like. And don't worry about finishing it all;

14

you're company." Her smile never wavered, bright and beautiful, though there was a firmness beneath it that dared him to argue.

"As for those two…" She glanced over at David and Tommy, who immediately straightened in their chairs, exchanging surprised looks. "They have to finish everything they put on their plates." She added the line with a quick wink at Christopher before returning to the kitchen.

He chuckled softly as he looked at David and Tommy, then took a bite of one of the biscuits. It practically melted in his mouth, sending him into a momentary dream-state, and then let out a soft sigh of pleasure.

After lunch, Katherine began clearing the table while the men leaned back in their chairs, content and full.

"Why is it that when a man eats a meal, he always has to hold or rub his stomach afterward?" she teased, directing the question at Christopher.

"Well, I'm not exactly sure," he said with a sheepish smile, touching his stomach, then pulling his hand away quickly.

"I ate just as much as everybody here, and I'm not holding my stomach." Katherine picked up the dishes and carried them to the sink. She reached for another plate. "So, I hear prom is next weekend. Do either of you have any surprise dates lined up?"

"Ah, come on, Mom! We're not going this year. The last two years were jinxed," Tommy replied, shaking his head.

"What was so bad about 'em?" David asked.

"Well, for starters, Dad, you chaperoned Christopher, me, and our dates in the station wagon from hell before either of us had driver's licenses. And last year, when I finally drove, everything was fine until Stephanie 'Upchuck' Olson threw up in the backseat."

"Yes, son, but it was still my station wagon."

"Yeah, but Tommy had to clean it up, so that made it his car, at least for that night," Christopher added with a laugh.

"Hey, watch it, man!" Tommy shot back.

"Well, at least your date said something," Christopher continued. "Mine was a mute. She didn't talk all night, except when we said it was time to go home, and then she just said, 'Good.'"

Katherine stopped and laughed. "Okay, so aren't y'all going to give it one last chance? You know it's the last prom you'll be able to go to," she said, wiping crumbs from the table.

"Well, I don't know, Mrs. Pri…" Christopher began, quickly correcting himself. "Excuse me, Katherine."

She smiled.

"It's just that we'd want the most perfect dates we

could get, being that it's our last year and all."

"My point exactly," she said, nodding. She continued cleaning the table off while carrying dishes to the kitchen. "Y'all need to go because it *is* your last year. You need to go regardless of who you're with. Just have fun. It's your last chance to be a kid."

Christopher listened intently, his eyes fixed on her as she spoke. For a moment, the comfort of her voice dulled the unease in his chest. Then David's leg struck the table. Suddenly, a glass slipped and fell, shattering across the floor. The sharp crack triggered something in Christopher's head, ripping through him, and he flinched as if the sword from his dream had struck stone again.

"Are you okay?" Katherine asked. "Christopher?"

"Yes," he replied, his voice subdued, but he was shaking. His hand drifted to his temple, as if he could push away the echo of the dream still ringing in his skull.

"Yo, Chris!" Tommy called out, trying to lighten the mood. "This wouldn't have anything to do with that dream you were going on about earlier, would it?"

He turned slowly to face Tommy, questioning if that was the reason.

"Christopher, what's wrong?" Katherine asked gently, touching his shoulder. "You look like you've seen a ghost."

"No, Mom, he just had a bad dream last night. He's

tough," Tommy said.

"Well, I know when something's bothering someone," she said. "And I also know that he's usually more upbeat than he's been today." She paused, and looked at Tommy, now serious. "But I also know when two teenage boys have something private between them, so I'll just tend to clean up that broken glass."

"Katherine, don't start cleaning up something that was clearly my fault," David said, standing up. "I'll take care of this mess, and then I'll help you finish up in the kitchen."

She nodded and returned to the kitchen. David gestured towards Christopher, signaling Tommy to help him.

Tommy noticed that Christopher was pale and sweating. His face had turned a dull ivory, damp with perspiration. "Say, Chris, why don't we go outside and get some fresh air?"

He was already staring at Tommy, pleading for a way out. "Yeah, I think that's a good idea."

He placed both hands on the table and tried to stand. It felt like he was trying to lift a freight train off his body. As he struggled, the table shook, catching David's attention.

His hand slipped, but Tommy was quick to steady him, slipping an arm under his to help him up. "Whoa. I got you, big guy. Let's go out to the patio," Tommy said.

David watched them go, and Katherine came back, standing by his side.

"Something's not right," she said quietly.

David didn't answer. His jaw tightened, but his eyes stayed on the door, as if he too had felt the weight of whatever haunted Christopher.

5

The early afternoon sun shone bright overhead, and shadows lay across the driveway when Tommy and Christopher stepped outside. The air was warm, carrying the scent of fresh-cut grass and the sound of children playing in a nearby park.

Tommy gently let go of Christopher, who had been sweating profusely. His shirt clung damp to his back, the kind of sweat that came from nerves, not heat. Trying to mask his own worry, Tommy casually wiped his hand on the back of his jeans.

Christopher ran a shaky hand through his hair, his breath coming in uneven gasps. "God, I'm fucked up! Did you see me in there? I must have looked like a fool. Your parents probably think I'm crazy now," he blurted out, his voice tinged with panic. The unsettling images from his dream still swimming in his head, and the strange sensation that had gripped him during lunch refused to loosen its hold on his mind.

Tommy leaned against the side of the house; the brick felt hot against his shoulder. He tried to maintain a calm demeanor despite the gnawing unease in his gut. He had never seen Christopher so unhinged and so vulnerable.

"Hey, man, take it easy. Just tell me what's going on," he replied. His voice was steady, but his heart pounded with worry.

Christopher's gaze drifted into the distance as he tried to piece together his thoughts. The sound of a car door slamming across the street made him jump, and he cursed under his breath.

"I'm telling you Tommy, something's wrong. I really think it has something to do with that damn dream I had," he said, his voice quivering. The dream felt like more than just a product of his subconscious; it felt like a warning, a premonition of something terrible.

"You seemed fine during lunch. Then suddenly you were a different person," Tommy said, still trying to make sense of what had happened. He crossed his arms, leaning in slightly as if being closer to Christopher might help him understand better. "It's like something flipped a switch in your head."

"When your dad knocked that glass off the table, it

probably just sounded like a regular glass breaking to you. But to me, it was like a gunshot. It was so loud, and... well, this is embarrassing, but my shorts are a little wet from the shock," he admitted, his cheeks flushing with humiliation, and still hearing the sound echoing in his head.

Tommy's eyebrows stood up in surprise, and he instinctively took a small step back. He knew his friend wasn't one to exaggerate, but this was something else.

"Tommy, please," Christopher said, pleading. "I know this sounds crazy, and I'm not asking you to believe me right away. But I need you to trust me enough to hear me out before you decide I belong in the nut house."

Tommy threw his hands up in mock surrender, trying to lighten the mood, but inside, his heart was racing. "Ah, I knew it! You're trying to drag me into this! I knew it!" he said, half-joking. But the truth was, he wasn't joking. He was scared.

Christopher laughed, though it was more of a nervous laugh than anything else. "Okay, maybe I said that wrong. I'm not trying to drag you into anything, I'm just asking," he said, trying to regain some sense of normalcy. But the weight in his chest refused to lift, and the fear gnawed at the edges of his mind.

Tommy looked at his friend, really looked at him, and saw the desperation in his eyes. This wasn't just some passing thing.

"Look, man," Tommy began, trying to recap everything in his head. "You showed up this morning looking depressed or scared, maybe both. Then you told me about that dream, the whole green eyes in the dark, and angels on fire with a sword. Then you heard a single word. Have I missed anything?"

"So far, so good," Christopher said, nodding. He appreciated that Tommy was taking this seriously, even if it seemed a little farfetched.

"Then we had lunch with my parents, like we've done a million times before. Then, my dad accidentally knocks a glass off the table, and you freak out, telling me you heard gunshots in your head."

Tommy's voice was steady, but there was an undercurrent of disbelief. How could all of this be connected? It didn't make any sense.

"That about covers it," Christopher said, stuffing his hands into his pockets and rocking back and forth on his toes, a grin playing on his lips. He knew how insane this all sounded, but he couldn't shake the feeling that something terrible was coming.

Tommy stared at him, feeling a mix of disbelief and worry. He had always thought Christopher had his head on straight. They were best friends, and Tommy cared deeply about him, but this situation was unsettling. He didn't know how to help. How do you help someone who might be losing it? Do you sit with him and keep quiet, hoping it passes? Do you press for answers and risk pushing him further? Tommy's mind raced with possibilities, none of them comforting. He wanted to help, but he was terrified that anything he did might make things worse. All Tommy knew was that he wanted his friend to get better so they could go back to being carefree seventeen-year-olds.

Looking into Christopher's eyes, Tommy saw genuine fear. It was unsettling to realize that Christopher was just as scared as he was, if not more so.

"Look, I'll do whatever I can to help, but try not to freak out on me again. It really scared me, okay?" Tommy said. His voice wavered slightly, betraying his own fear.

"Deal," Christopher agreed, relieved to have someone on his side. But the relief was short-lived as the weight of the situation settled back over him like a shroud.

Tommy looked up at the sky, squinting against the brightness. The warm air carried a faint breeze, and it reminded him of the afternoons they used to spend camping out in his backyard, talking into the night and telling ghost stories until they were too scared to sleep. He missed those simpler times when the scariest thing they had to worry about was a raccoon rummaging through their food.

"Hey, how about we go cruise around for a while?" Tommy suggested, hoping to lighten the mood, and thinking some fresh air and the open road would help clear their heads.

"Sounds good," Christopher said, grateful for the distraction.

Tommy threw his arm around his best friend, pulling him close for a moment before letting go. "We'll figure this out, Chris. Whatever it is, we'll figure it out."

Together they walked toward the garage.

The Mustang waited like an old friend, its chrome catching the sunlight.

Tommy dangled the keys in front of Christopher, smiling. "Why don't you drive for a while? Might help take your mind off things."

Christopher nodded, sliding behind the wheel. He turned the key, and the engine roared to life. He cranked up the radio, and the music filled the car, filling the void between them.

As they backed out of the driveway and headed down the street, the wind whipped through the open windows, carrying away the tension. Christopher leaned into the wheel, the sun bright in his eyes, and the fresh air cooling his face.

Tommy looked at his friend, relieved to see some of the tension easing. "You know, we've been through a lot together, Chris. I don't care what's going on with you. I'm here for you no matter what. You've got to remember that, okay?"

Christopher could hear the sincerity in his friend's voice, and it brought a lump to his throat. "I know, Tommy. I don't know what I'd do without you, man."

"Good thing you don't have to find out," Tommy said with a grin, punching Christopher lightly on the arm.

The sunlight flashed across the hood and the heat shimmered on the asphalt. They drove aimlessly, the town blurring past in waves of glass storefronts and traffic lights. The world outside seemed distant, almost unreal, as if they were the only two people left in existence.

The open road had a way of making his problems seem smaller, more manageable. The familiar hum of the engine and the steady rhythm of the tires on the pavement were like a lullaby, soothing his frayed nerves.

After a while, they pulled over, and Tommy slid behind the wheel. Christopher leaned back in the passenger seat, content to let his friend take over.

Tommy guided the Mustang back onto the road; the engine purred under his touch. Christopher felt better as he settled deeper into the seat.

For a while, they drove in silence, the only sound coming from under the hood and the occasional call of a bird from the fields along the roadside. As the afternoon wore on, Christopher found himself relaxing more and more. The fear that had gripped him earlier seemed like a distant memory, something he could barely recall. But deep down, he knew it wasn't gone. It was still there, a cold knot of dread in the pit of his stomach, waiting for the right moment to strike.

He looked at Tommy and knew his friend was just as tired as he was, but Tommy had always been the stronger one, the one who could push through when things got tough. Christopher envied that about him and wished he could be more like that.

"Thanks for this, Tommy," he said.

"Anytime, Chris. You know that."

They drove on, the road stretching out before them like an endless ribbon. For the first time in what felt like forever, Christopher allowed himself to hope that maybe, just maybe, things would be okay. But even in that flicker of hope, something darker loomed, reminding him it wasn't over, not by a long shot.

6

Tommy maneuvered the Mustang into a spot in the crowded mall parking lot, easing the car into place with the practiced hand of someone who took pride in his vehicle. The lot was alive with the kind of Saturday afternoon buzz that seemed to draw everyone from their high school into the open air. People loitered between cars, and the conversations of many blended.

Christopher glanced around, sweeping the parking lot. "I thought we were just gonna cruise?" he asked, a slight edge of disappointment in his voice.

Tommy shifted his gaze from the rearview mirror to Christopher, adjusting his hair. "I'd rather check out girls. Besides, I'm running low on gas."

Christopher laughed. "No kidding, you've been driving like Mach 1 the whole way here."

Silence followed. Tommy searched his friend's face, thinking, *You okay, man?* though the words never left his mouth.

Christopher forced a smile, the corners of his mouth lifting just enough to reassure him. "Hey, I'm sorry. I guess I'm just freaking out. You're right, let's go walk around. It'll do me some good." He extended his hand toward Tommy. "Still buds?"

Tommy smacked his palm playfully. "You bet, weiser."

The familiar nickname broke the tension, and Christopher laughed this time. Tommy wasn't just a friend, he was like a brother.

Inside the mall, a wave of cool, recycled air rushed over Christopher, a relief from the heat outside. The sudden chill raised goosebumps on his arms. He inhaled deeply, taking in the mix of different scents from inside. The air was laced with popcorn, cinnamon, and even a hint of perfume escaped from a nearby kiosk. The corridors bustled with families pushing strollers, groups of kids shoving and laughing, and couples drifting hand in hand. The tinny strains of elevator music were piped in overhead, riding just below the chaos of voices.

Christopher tried to let the atmosphere steady him, to let the normalcy sink in to calm his nerves. But it wasn't that simple. He could not shake the dream from his head.

It clung to him like a shadow. Every light seemed too bright, and every voice was too sharp. He realized the mall wasn't helping him; it was amplifying the problem.

As they made their way up the escalator, Christopher leaned over the railing. Below, in the center court, was a large, glossy black piano. It was filling the spot where a fountain usually sat. A pianist played a classical piece; the notes rose delicately into the open air. It felt a little out of place against the music coming from overhead, along with the backdrop of chatter and foot traffic.

Before Christopher could lose himself in the music, Tommy nudged him.

"Hey, isn't that girl in your world history class?" he asked, nodding toward the lower level.

Christopher's gaze followed. The moment his eyes landed on the girl, a chill ran through him. The hair on his neck bristled.

"Yeah," he said, voice tight. "Her name's Claudia. I don't remember her last name."

Tommy raised an eyebrow. "She's good-looking. Why don't you ask her to prom?"

Christopher rubbed the back of his neck, trying to ease the sudden tension. "I think somebody already has." He nodded toward the guy standing close to her.

The guy stared back, his expression hard, daring Tommy to make the first move.

His name was Hector Lopez, known by everyone as Spidy. He had a black widow tattoo crawling from wrist to thumb, a mark that had made him infamous. The story was legend.

It was their freshman year, a senior pulled a knife on him. Spidy tripped the guy, and the blade landed in Spidy's hand, and in one wild second, he had the senior pinned, with the knife to his throat. It had been more accident than intention, but the story spread until Spidy's name carried weight. Truth was, he hadn't been in a real fight since. Tommy knew the truth; he'd been there that day, his locker was only two down from Spidy's.

Their eyes were still locked, and the memory thick between them. Claudia touched Hector's arm, whispering something to calm him, but his glare stayed fixed on Tommy.

"What do you think she's saying?" Christopher asked.

"Who knows," Tommy said with a shrug, smirking at Hector. Then Tommy cupped his hands around his mouth, and shouted, "Heeeecctoooorrrr!" His middle finger shot into the air. The bold challenge rang across both floors.

Christopher's heart sank. Once Tommy locked onto something, there was no stopping him.

Hector moved instantly, shoving through people on the lower level, eyes burning with fury. The mall seemed to pause, heads turned between Tommy above and Hector below like spectators at a match.

Tommy grinned and bolted for the down escalator. As he ran, he hissed to Christopher, "Go get your girl."

Christopher froze at the railing as Tommy thundered down the moving steps, taking them two at a time. Hector waited at the bottom, and the second Tommy leapt off, Hector lunged. Tommy twisted away, laughing, and sprinted across the floor. Shoppers scattered as the chase carved a wild path through kiosks and startled families.

Reluctantly, Christopher descended after them. He spotted Claudia glaring his way with her arms folded tight. His heart hammered as he crossed toward her. The noise from the mall pushed against him, feeling claustrophobic. Behind him, the clamor of Tommy and Hector's pursuit ricocheted like a cartoon come to life.

"You know, you've got a pretty stupid friend," Claudia said as he approached.

"Oh yeah? Why's that?"

"Because Hector will tear him apart if he catches him."

Her disdain for Tommy was clear, and the weight of Hector's hatred was obvious.

Tommy streaked past them in a blur, his voice carrying: "Did you ask her?" Hector barreled after him, face tight with determination.

"Did you ask me what?" Claudia snapped, stepping closer. She was striking and confident, with an edge that made Christopher feel like she might flatten him on the spot.

Before he could answer, a harsh discord sounded from the piano. He glanced around and saw Tommy sprawled across the keys, Hector was closing in as the pianist stormed away.

"Ask me what?" Claudia demanded, dragging his attention back.

The words tumbled out before he could stop them. "I wanted to ask if you didn't have a date yet, if you'd like to go to prom?"

Her sternness softened into a smile.

Encouraged, he added, "And maybe bring a friend for Tommy."

She burst out laughing, loud and sharp. "You've got to be kidding me!"

"Look, uh—"

"Claudia. Claudia Montgomery. Don't forget it, asshole."

She grabbed his jacket lapels and yanked him close. Instinctively, he shoved her hands off.

"Don't grab me like that."

"Don't ask me out," she shot back.

"Don't worry, I wouldn't want to have to put you on a

leash," he snapped, then turned away.

Her face flushed red. She clawed the side of his neck, nails digging deep. He yelped, pulling forward.

"Listen!" he shouted. "I asked you out, you turned me down, so I got sarcastic. No need to claw my head off!"

Her fist flew, connecting with his eye. He staggered, checked for blood, then caught her foot as she kicked. She hopped on one leg, screaming, "Let go!"

He twisted, and dropped her hard to the side.

At the same instant, Tommy vaulted past again with Hector close behind. Hector tripped and crashed face-first into Claudia, the two of them collapsing in a twisted knot.

Security whistles screamed. "Hey, kids! Stop!"

Christopher grabbed Tommy's arm. "Come on, let's get out of here!"

Tommy, laughing wildly, ran backward as Christopher pulled him. Guards converged, one stopping to untangle Hector and Claudia, while the other ran after the boys.

Christopher glanced back.

Claudia shoved the guard's hands away, shouting, "I'm fine! Don't touch me!" Then her eyes locked on Christopher. The mall blurred, sound warped, and the air around her bent, her voice slid into his head like ice water.

You're mine, a voice whispered in his head.

He paused, realizing it was her. Without thinking, he shot back silently, *Come and get it.*

Her expression faltered. She'd heard him.

"Come on!" Tommy barked, dragging him toward the up escalator.

They bounded upward, pushing past startled shoppers.

Christopher looked once more. Claudia stood below, brushing herself off, her gaze still locked to his. He forced himself to break eye contact and follow Tommy.

They burst through the glass doors into the heat of the afternoon. The sound of the mall faded behind them, but the chill crawling up Christopher's spine stayed with him. He didn't need to look back to know Claudia was still watching.

And she was.

7

Tommy and Christopher drove home in silence. The Mustang's engine seemed louder now, amplifying the tension hanging in the air between them.

Tommy's thoughts raced as he gripped the steering wheel. He couldn't shake the image of Hector charging after him through the mall, something he knew he had brought on himself. And he couldn't forget the haunted look in Christopher's eyes after the encounter with Claudia.

The Mustang pulled into the garage and rumbled to a stop, leaving a hollow silence floating in the air. It began to tick, cooling down after a long afternoon. Twilight was fading fast, and the last remnants of daylight cast shadows across the interior of the car. The small crystal pyramid hanging from the rearview mirror caught the dying light, scattering fractured beams of color across the dashboard. Normally, it was a comforting sight, a reminder of the countless rides they had taken together. But now, it only seemed to deepen the sense of unease gnawing at Tommy.

Christopher remained motionless in the passenger seat; his eyes stared blankly ahead. He was trying to process everything that had happened, but his thoughts were tangled, knotted up in a way that made them impossible to unravel. The encounter with Claudia had left him shaken, because of the uncanny connection he had felt with her. It was as if she had reached into his mind, planting thoughts that weren't entirely his own. And that connection terrified him more than he was willing to admit.

Finally, he faced Tommy, who was already watching him with concern etched across his face. "I'm okay, you know," Christopher said quietly, though he wasn't sure if he was trying to convince Tommy or himself.

Tommy raised an eyebrow. "Oh sure, because it's totally normal to plan on asking a beautiful girl out and end up in a fight with her. Meanwhile, your best friend is risking his life for you."

Christopher rolled his eyes and looked away, feeling the sting of Tommy's words more deeply than he let on.

"But hey, you did your best," Tommy continued, his tone lightening, while a smirk played on his lips. "Though

I was particularly impressed with the staring contest there at the end."

Christopher let out a sigh. "Ah, come on, man. Calm down," he muttered, rubbing his temples as if trying to erase the memory of the whole fiasco.

Tommy wasn't done, though. He leaned back in his seat, his grin widening. "No, really. I want to know what that was all about. Dazzle me."

Christopher hesitated. How could he explain something he didn't fully understand himself? But Tommy was his best friend, if he couldn't confide in him, then who could he trust?

He gave in. "Dazzle you? Fine. I don't really get it either, but I thought she was speaking to me."

Tommy frowned. "What, like with body language or some kind of secret code?"

Christopher shook his head, "Okay, I didn't expect you to understand," he admitted. "But I'm willing to try and explain. You said you'd listen, remember?"

Tommy nodded, "All right, give it another shot."

Christopher took a deep breath, trying to piece everything together.

"So maybe she wasn't actually talking to me, but it sure felt like it," he began, his voice steady but uncertain. "I swear I thought I heard her say, 'You're mine,' like she was right next to me. And for some reason, I just responded, 'Come and get it,' or at least, I think I did. Maybe it was just in my head. I don't know," he said, rubbing his temples again.

Tommy listened carefully, trying to make sense of it all. "I never said you were lying. It's just… a lot to take in. But don't worry, I believe you." He extended his hand, and Christopher grasped it firmly, the familiar gesture bringing a small measure of comfort.

"We're friends to the end, Chris."

Christopher looked at him, the weight of his friend's words settling over him like a warm blanket. "You mean it?"

"Of course. Always, no matter what." Tommy's voice was resolute, and for the first time since they left the mall, Christopher felt better. Maybe they could figure this out together. Maybe things *would* go back to normal, or at least something close to it.

Tommy reached for the driver's door, pushing it open and letting the faint dome light cast a soft yellow glow on their faces. "You need some sleep, and so do I. Try to get some rest and call me tomorrow. Maybe we can figure this out together, okay?"

"Yeah, okay."

As he got out of the car and walked toward his house, he felt a wave of depression and discouragement wash over him, threatening to pull him under. He didn't want to worry Tommy any more than he already had.

Tommy watched him go, leaning against the back of the Mustang as he called out, "Keep your chin up!"

Christopher turned his head toward Tommy's voice, lifting a thumb in the air.

A knot of worry tightened in Tommy's chest. He knew something was seriously wrong, but he also knew that pushing Christopher too hard might only make things worse. With a sigh, he turned and headed inside to get some rest, hoping that tomorrow would bring some clarity.

Christopher reached his front porch and paused, breathing in the cool night air. The night was quiet, broken only by the rustling of leaves in the breeze. The porch swing waited, swaying gently. He lowered himself onto the wooden seat; it creaked under his weight, then leaned back to stare at the stars. They sparkled like scattered diamonds across the sky, but even their brilliance couldn't lift the heaviness that weighed on his mind.

The swing rocked gently as he pushed off with his foot. Claudia's face replayed in his mind, the way she had looked at him, with that intensity in her eyes. It was too much, telling himself it was just stress.

Closing his eyes, he let the breeze wash over him. Instead of clarity, more questions surfaced. Why had she felt so familiar, as if they had met before? And why had he answered her with his mind, challenging her?

The swing's creak became a lullaby, pulling him toward sleep. The turmoil inside him remained, but exhaustion was stronger. His eyelids grew heavy, and the stars blurred above him.

As he drifted off, the voice returned, soft and insistent, echoing from the corners of his mind:

You're mine.

Christopher stirred, a frown crossing his face, but the swing carried him deeper into slumber. The porch was quiet, and the stars kept silent watch as unease settled into his dreams.

8

In the dead of night, a high, piercing neigh split the air, rousing the sheriff from his doze. The rain was coming down hard, though he wasn't sure how long it had been pouring. The streets were a muddy mess, and the downpour drummed relentlessly on the rooftops. Across the street, the saloon's windows glowed faintly, while patrons peered out at the brawl unfolding in the muck outside.

The sheriff had kept the peace in Harlequin, Texas, for five years without fail, and he intended to keep it that way tonight. It had been one of those slow, almost boring nights, and the sheriff had nodded off in his favorite spot… the rocking chair in front of the jail.

He wasn't married anymore, that was a different story. His wife had been killed on their first day in town, caught in the crossfire as some men escaped from jail. After that, he stayed, becoming the sheriff to maintain order in the town that had taken her from him.

Buddy "Slim" Rysack had just finished pummeling an old man into the mud. The sheriff had been watching, thinking he'd let them brawl for a few minutes before stepping in. He figured he'd send the old drifter on his way with a free drink, and then lock Buddy up for the night.

With a sigh of disgust, he shook his head. "Won't they ever learn?" he muttered to himself as he stood up.

He threw on his poncho, adjusted his hat, and stepped out into the downpour. The mud sucked at his boots with every step, the rain hammering down even harder now that he was out in it.

As he approached the group ahead, the sheriff recognized some familiar faces: Davy Hackett, Clay Young, Buddy Rysack, and Danny Owens, Buddy's sidekick. The old man was still down on one knee in the mud, someone the sheriff had never seen before. He could hear Buddy yelling as he got closer.

"Don't you ever touch my cards again! And my drink! Where do you come from? Drinking out of my glass! Answer me, old man!" Buddy screamed in the man's face, nearly touching noses together.

"Take it easy, Buddy," the sheriff said as he joined the half-circle of onlookers, looking down at the stranger. He had locked Buddy up so many times for drunken brawls that they were practically on a first-name basis.

"Sheriff, I've had enough! This old fool came in here…"

Buddy's voice trailed off as the old man looked up at the sheriff, a familiar glint in his eyes that made the sheriff pause.

"…and he grabs one of my playing cards right out of my hand. Then he takes my glass, puts it to his filthy mouth, and drinks all my whiskey! I didn't start nothin' this time, sheriff. Hell, I ain't even drunk! I walked out here, didn't I?"

"That you did," the sheriff replied, his eyes still fixed on the man. "What've you got to say for yourself, drifter?"

The man wiped blood from the corner of his mouth and looked up at Buddy, who towered over him like a giant. To Buddy, the old man looked like a mutt that needed a lesson. But instead of fear, the stranger's lips curled into a smile.

"What are you looking at?" Buddy shouted, his anger rising. The drifter's smile widened, and a soft laugh escaped his lips.

"I believe he's laughing at you, Buddy," Danny Owens said.

Buddy shot Danny a glare. "I can hear 'em!"

"Now come on, folks," the sheriff intervened, "let's all

head back inside and work this out where it's dry."

"Not just yet," Buddy snarled, grabbing a fistful of the man's hair, and yelling. "*What* are you laughing at?"

"Because you're still gonna have that same shit-eating grin on your face when you're dead," the stranger replied through his laughter.

Buddy's face shifted with disbelief, maybe fear, then hardened into rage as the old man's laughter grew louder.

"Now, Buddy, don't do anything stupid," the sheriff warned. "Let's just go inside, and I'll buy everyone a drink."

But Buddy wasn't listening, and neither were the others. They were all fixated on Buddy's reddening face as he drew back his right foot, ready to kick. But as he swung his leg forward, the old man caught it with his left hand, his laughter abruptly ceasing.

In a flash, the old man pulled out a knife, a long, gleaming Argentine gaucho blade, and thrust it into Buddy's gut, right below his navel. The men around them recoiled in shock, backing away as Buddy staggered, his hands instinctively searching for the knife's handle. The sheriff's eyes widened in disbelief. Why hadn't he stopped this? Why couldn't he move?

Buddy stared down at the knife protruding from his abdomen, the reality of it slowly sinking in. The drifter, still crouched on one knee, gripped the handle with both hands. With a sudden heave, he rose to his feet, dragging the blade upward in a powerful thrust that split Buddy open, the steel ripping through flesh and muscle until it stopped mid-chest. Standing over him now, the man locked eyes with Buddy, his grip unyielding on the buried knife.

Blood poured out, soaking the mud and splattering his boots.

Buddy's body convulsed, his hands trembled as the drifter plunged his fist into the gaping wound, their eyes locked the entire time. With a grimace, he twisted his arm, digging deeper, searching with slow precision until Buddy felt something tear loose inside him.

Buddy's eyes bulged, terror reflected back at him in the drifter's unblinking stare. The man slowly pulled his hand free, holding something dark red and pulsing—Buddy's heart. Still staring into him, he raised it for Buddy to see. Buddy's vision darkened, then the world slipped away.

Buddy collapsed into the mud, lifeless.

The figure stood over him, holding the heart that continued to twitch in his hand.

The sheriff remained frozen, as if the rain itself had turned to chains around his body. He knew that anything he did would be useless.

The old man dropped the heart into the mud and,

without a word, began walking away. The crowd parted for him, avoiding his gaze. As he passed the sheriff, he placed a twenty-dollar gold piece in his hand. "I'll be leavin' town now."

The sheriff folded his fingers around the coin and nodded, his eyes fixed on Buddy's lifeless body. The old man touched the sheriff below the chin, guiding his eyes back to attention, then winked at him. Something stirred in the sheriff's memory. He knew this man, but from where?

The man leaned in, stopping inches from the sheriff's face. In a voice that didn't match his weathered appearance, a woman's voice, he asked, "How's your neck, Christopher?"

It was her. It was Claudia! But how was she in this dream? *I am dreaming, right?* the sheriff thought, staring into the old man's eyes.

The man reached behind the sheriff's neck, pulling him close, and kissed him passionately.

The sheriff tried to resist, but the old man's grip was too strong. He felt teeth sink into his tongue, the taste of blood filling his mouth.

The old man bit down harder.

Christopher jolted awake. His eyes flew open, and he found himself staring at the wooden ceiling of the front porch. Cobwebs clung to the corners where the roof met the walls. It hadn't been just a dream. Coughing and gagging, he shot up, spitting blood onto the porch between his feet as his head hung low.

He tried to recall the dream, but it eluded him. All he could remember was the kiss just before waking. But now, exhausted and with his tongue throbbing from where he'd nearly bitten it in half, he didn't care. He needed sleep.

As the bleeding stopped, Christopher stood, taking one last look at the night sky before heading inside. He closed the door behind him, ready for a night without dreams.

9

The morning air was crisp, sitting at sixty-nine degrees. It was the kind of morning that felt charged with possibilities, even if the day ahead promised nothing more than routine.

The school parking lot was alive, humming with the restless energy of teenagers clustering in small groups. Girls leaned in close, whispering about who was dating whom, and what the latest rumors were that filled the halls the day before. Their faces were lit with excitement, as if every secret belonged to them alone.

The boys moved differently, gathering in wide circles that gave them room to posture. Their clothing carried the practiced look of carelessness, sneakers spotless and gleaming like trophies. They laughed louder, and traded jabs that cut deeper than they let on. From open car doors, bass-heavy rap rolled out, shaking the ground beneath them and setting the rhythm for the morning.

In the shadows, something else passed unnoticed by most. Small bottles changed hands. Pills were pressed into waiting palms. A flash of metal moved between two boys in the far corner, quick and discreet. The lot was its own marketplace, its own underworld, layered beneath the chatter and the laughter.

Hector leaned against the bumper of his Cutlass Supreme, the car polished to a shine that threw the sun back in sharp reflections. Blue flames curled up the maroon hood and crawled down the sides, a detail that drew eyes whether he wanted them or not. The stereo pounded out of the trunk, bass deep enough to rattle windows across the lot. Hector stood with one hand on his beer and the other resting on the car, his eyes steady on the scene around him.

Dushaun crossed the lot with his usual swagger, cigarette tucked behind his ear. He pulled it free as he approached, slipping it into Hector's hand.

"Whasup, ma' man?" he said with a grin.

Hector nodded, sliding the cigarette behind his own ear. "Nothin'."

"So where's your girl?" Dushaun asked, scanning the crowd.

"Prob'ly late. Her mom was ridin' her again last night.

Doesn't want her around me."

"Shame. Can't even drive your girl to school."

Hector's jaw tightened. He took another pull from the bottle. "Fuck off. Go hassle somebody else."

Dushaun gave a mock salute, his smirk never fading, then wandered off into the crowd.

Hector watched him go, knowing better than to trust him. He turned back to the car and leaned against it once more.

The sound of an engine pulled his attention to the entrance of the lot. A car he recognized rolled in, and Claudia stepped out. For a moment, the noise and chatter around him fell away. She caught his eye as she closed the door, and the look she gave him was enough to still the rest of the morning.

Hector straightened, tossed his empty bottle into the trash, and walked to meet her halfway.

"Hey," he said, his voice softer than it had been a minute ago.

"Hey." Her eyes searched his face, cautious, as if still carrying her mother's warnings.

They stood there in the lot with the crowd moving around them and music playing, but neither of them heard it. The tension between them was the weight of what her mother thought of him. Hector felt it. For the first time that morning, he knew the balance had shifted. Something was changing, and once it tipped, nothing would return to the way it had been.

10

At 7:45 a.m., the Mustang rolled into the South entrance of the Martin High parking lot. Behind the wheel, Tommy was a different person, focused and intense. He wore mirrored sunglasses, claiming they were comfortable, but Christopher knew better. Tommy idolized the liquid metal man from the Terminator movie and often talked about how cool it would be to look and act like that.

Christopher leaned back in his seat, still feeling groggy despite a full night's sleep. Maybe it was too much sleep, or maybe he was just slowly going crazy. He couldn't shake the confusion swirling in his mind about Claudia and the anger toward him. He felt it was rooted from somewhere else, but couldn't understand it. On top of that, he still thought of the dream, the green eyes, and the angel. Now, his latest, some western town. He felt a wave of nausea and realized he needed food.

As Tommy parked the car, Christopher noticed a large group of students gathered at the North end of the parking lot. It wasn't unusual, just bigger than normal, and the center of attention seemed to be Hector's car. He slowly sat up to get a better look.

"There's your running mate, Tommy," Christopher said, his sarcasm thin.

"Very funny, lover boy," Tommy shot back, scanning the crowd over the top of his glasses. "Doesn't this crap get old for these guys? Standing around with the same music pounding in their ears?"

"I guess not."

"I mean, really. It's always the same. Then the hall monitor shows up on his little golf cart, breaks them up, and sends them inside like he's some kind of authority."

"Well, he can't do much else," Christopher pointed out.

"He could if he wanted to! He could bust them for weapons, drugs, disturbing the peace…"

"I think he's just trying to stay alive," Christopher said. "His job is to get everyone inside without too much trouble, not to get shot. Besides…" Christopher's voice faded. "Look, there he is… Tiger Woods."

"Where?" Tommy asked, still peering over his glasses.

"Over there, parked at the edge of the school."

Tommy followed his line of sight, squinting at the hall monitor who was indeed watching the scene from a distance.

"Look at him," Tommy muttered. "He's just gonna sit there and do nothing. He's scared. It's obvious."

"Well, shall we?" Christopher gestured toward the door, inviting Tommy to make the first move.

"No, Chris, the real question is, should we?"

They both eyed the large crowd, silently debating whether to wait for Hector and his followers to head inside before leaving the safety of the Mustang.

"Look at us," Tommy said, smacking Christopher lightly on the chest. "What are we, scared?"

They were, but neither would admit it.

"C'mon, we'll go now. We'll just walk through them and maybe get some weird looks or a few beer cans thrown at us," Tommy explained.

"Yeah right. As soon as we step out, you'll be off running another marathon with your buddy."

"Not this time. I'll stick with you, no matter what happens," Tommy replied, a sly grin on his face.

"Alright. Just stay cool."

"Let's do this." Tommy stashed his sunglasses in the glove box before opening his door.

Christopher crossed himself jokingly, then followed Tommy's lead, stepping out into the parking lot.

* * *

Hector opened another beer and noticed the black Mustang entering the lot, driving slowly. He knew who it was but couldn't figure out why they were driving so slow. As they parked, he watched them glance in his direction, then at each other, clearly trying to decide their next move. Hector knew this situation always meant something was about to go down.

He set his beer down carefully by his foot, never taking his eyes off the Mustang. As he walked away from his car, he spotted Dushaun dancing with a girl, who was sandwiched between him and another guy.

"Dushaun!"

Dushaun looked up, saw Hector approaching, and quickly bobbed his head in acknowledgment. "What's up, man?"

"Come here," Hector said, gesturing with his hand. Dushaun reassured the girl he'd be right back, then nudged her closer to his buddy.

"What's on your mind, Spidy?"

"That." Hector pointed toward the Mustang. "Guess who that is?"

"How would I know, man?"

"They're watching us too closely. I don't like it,"

Hector said, his tone growing serious.

"Do you want me to gather the troops and set up a perimeter, General?"

"Don't be a smartass. Something's up."

"Maybe they're just talking."

"Yeah, but I want to know what they're talking about," Hector said, his eyes narrowing. "Look at that. What's he pointing at?"

Dushaun saw the Mustang's passenger pointing toward the school. He followed the direction and spotted the hall monitor parked at the edge of the building, staring right back at them.

"He's pointing at the hall monitor," Dushaun said. "Maybe they're waiting for him to leave."

"No, I've got a bad feeling," Hector muttered.

"That's not good. Last time you had a bad feeling, I got shot at," Dushaun whined.

"Shut up! The door just opened," Hector snapped.

* * *

Tommy and Christopher stepped out of the Mustang and started walking toward the school. Hector felt the hair on his neck stand on end, and knew this was his time to do something about it.

"Do it," Hector ordered, tapping Dushaun on the

chest before ducking behind his car.

Dushaun raised his arm, making rapid circles with his index finger above his head while whistling loudly. Instantly, everyone in the group stopped what they were doing and took cover behind car doors, and anything else that provided protection. The laughter and bass cut off, swallowed by silence. The lot felt staged, like a silent arena waiting for blood.

Tommy and Christopher continued across the lot; Christopher's mind raced. His chest tightened, each step heavier than the last. He could feel eyes on him from every angle, the crowd folding around them like a trap. He glanced at Tommy, his eyes resembled Dirty Harry, studying the situation before the fight. When he looked back toward the sea of cars, it was clear they were surrounded. The once bustling group had grown legs and taken cover, ready for an ambush. *But don't worry,* Christopher thought sarcastically, *Tommy has a plan.*

His heart pounded as they reached the center of the cul-de-sac of cars. Suddenly, two more cars pulled in behind them, trapping them in the middle. Christopher immediately recognized the short Hispanic male walking toward them. He was dressed in a white tank top tucked into neatly pressed pants, and an open button-up shirt that flared with each gust of wind. It was then that Christopher noticed the gun tucked in his waistband.

"What's up? I think you gentlemen are in the wrong place at the right time. Know what I mean?" Hector said, clasping his hands in front of him like a politician.

Tommy sprang to life. "No, man, you're in the wrong place at the right…"

But then, everything seemed to slow down. Christopher knew the word Tommy was struggling to finish… *time*, but he never got the chance to say it.

Christopher's eyes locked on Hector. The smile was gone. Time seemed to stretch as he turned to see what everyone else was focused on. Then a fist crashed into Tommy's face, snapping his nose sideways with a sickening crack. Blood streamed instantly, and Christopher cringed in horror.

"What are you people doing?!" he shouted, his voice trembling as he looked at his fallen friend. Rage surged in him; he wanted to lunge at Hector, but fear rooted him in place.

Hector only smiled, calm again. "Well, your friend has other things to worry about now instead of helping you out of this mess."

Tommy was kneeling on the ground, clutching his broken nose.

Christopher turned back to Hector, who was shaking his head in mock disappointment. Hector's eyes shifted to something behind him, but before he could react, Hector leaned in close and whispered, "Sweet dreams, lover boy."

Christopher felt a sharp pain in his lower back. Everything in front of him began to blur, and his vision narrowed until all he could see was Hector's face, slowly fading into darkness. He dropped to his knees, then collapsed onto his side, unconscious.

11

Ms. Hawthorne meticulously arranged the contents of her son's lunchbox, as if each item held the key to his well-being. The PB&J sandwich was the first to go in, its crusts neatly trimmed and packed with care. Beside it, she placed a thermos filled with homemade chicken noodle soup, ensuring the lid was secured. Next, a small packet of crackers, an apple polished to a shine, and finally, a small carton of 2% low-fat milk.

As she closed the lunchbox, a pang of sorrow washed over her. Life as a single mother hadn't been easy, and there were nights when the weight of it nearly crushed her. She often found herself wondering if she was doing enough for Christopher, now ten years old. The hardest part was knowing he had no father figure to look back on, and that thought ate at her.

Her thoughts were interrupted by the sound of hurried footsteps as he burst into the kitchen.

"Mom, is my lunch ready yet?" he asked, his voice full of the impatience that only a child could muster.

"Just finishing it up. Here you go," she replied, handing him the lunchbox with a warm smile. For a moment she just watched him, struck by how tall he was getting, and how fast time was pulling him away.

"Give me a kiss before you go," she requested, her voice gentle yet firm.

"Ah, come on, Mom. Do we always have to do this?" Christopher groaned, though there was no real annoyance in his tone, just the faint embarrassment of a child growing up.

"Now, don't be like that. I thought you only didn't like it when I did this in front of your friends?"

She leaned down and planted a kiss on his right cheek, drawing it out with an exaggerated "mmmahhh" sound that made him squirm.

"Gross, Mom," he protested, wiping his cheek.

"Have fun at school, and stay out of trouble," she said, knowing full well that her son was prone to a little mischief.

"You know I always do," Christopher replied with a grin as he dashed out the back door with infectious energy.

"I love you."

"I love you too!" He was already halfway down the path.

He might have hated the kisses, but hearing those words made it all worthwhile for her. She knew the affection would come in time; for now, she just had to be patient and cherish the small moments they shared.

She wanted to believe that everything would be okay, that she was doing enough as both mother and father. But as she returned to her morning chores, a small voice in the back of her mind whispered doubts.

Christopher loved walking to school. The air was crisp this morning beneath a clear blue sky. He drew in a deep breath, and filled his lungs with the scent of dew and cool soil. Each morning, as he set out on the familiar path, he let his imagination run wild, transforming the ordinary streets and fields into a vast, magical landscape where he was the hero. He pictured battlefields in his head, monsters hiding in ditches, or finding treasure behind chain-link fences. In his mind, he was a great warrior on a mission, defeating fierce enemies, and rescuing beautiful damsels in distress. He could almost hear the clash of swords and the roar of dragons as he made his way toward the large field that surrounded his school.

Lost in his daydreams, Christopher was suddenly jolted back to reality by a glint of something in the grass. He stopped in his tracks when he spotted the object. It caught the sun like a shard of ice, out of place in the weeds.

He crouched down to get a closer look, his curiosity piqued. The object was a necklace, unlike any he had ever seen before. The chain looked to be made of solid silver, with large, heavy links that gleamed with an almost otherworldly sheen. As he reached down to pick it up, a small shock ran through his fingers, making him jump back in surprise. But the shock only made him more determined to examine it further.

Tentatively, he reached out again and managed to grasp the necklace without incident. It was surprisingly heavy, as if it had been made for someone much larger than himself. The necklace felt important, as if it had been waiting for him, and he already felt a strong desire to keep it.

The chain was about twenty-four inches long, and at the end of it hung a strange medallion. The medallion was unique. It was heavy like stone but had the appearance of glass, smooth and cool to the touch. In the center of the stone, or glass, was something that looked like a drop of bright blue liquid, suspended as if by magic. Surrounding the blue drop were what appeared to be nerve-like strands, radiating outward toward the surface of the medallion, giving it an eerie, almost living quality.

Then it dawned on him. It was an eye. Or at least, it

resembled one, though it was far too large to be a real eye. As Christopher stared into it, mesmerized, something extraordinary happened. He noticed the blue liquid moving, starting to swirl. The more it moved, the more it felt like it was watching him.

He decided to wear it for the rest of the walk to school. He slipped the necklace over his head, and felt the weight of it settle against his chest. He figured he would take it off and hide it in his backpack when he got to school, then examine it more closely when he got home. For now, though, he wanted to keep it close, to feel its strange, comforting presence.

As he continued his walk, he couldn't shake the feeling that the necklace was somehow alive, aware of him. It was an unsettling thought, but one that only added to the necklace's allure. He found himself touching it frequently, running his fingers along the smooth surface of the medallion. Every touch made his stomach twist, half comfort, half dread.

The school loomed ahead, its brick walls and tall windows were stark against the bright sky. Normally, Christopher would have been focused on the day ahead, but today, all he could think about was the necklace. Who had it belonged to? And why did it feel like it belonged to *him* now?

At the entrance, he slipped it off and tucked it into his

backpack. Even so, the weight lingered, as if the medallion still rested on him.

The day passed in a blur. He barely heard his teachers, his mind circled back to the necklace. By the final bell he was restless, eager to be alone with it again.

As he walked home, clouds rolled in, a storm threatening the horizon. He barely noticed. His pace quickened until he was through the door. He brushed past his mother's hello and rushed to his room.

He pulled the necklace from his backpack and held it up to the light. The medallion glowed faintly in the dimness and the blue liquid swirled.

A chill spread through him. It wasn't just jewelry. It was something older, something awake. As he stared into it, a thought struck him cold. Whatever it was, it had chosen him.

12

Christopher felt a strange sense of detachment as the security guard carefully placed the oxygen mask over his face. The man's voice reached him through a haze, muffled and distant, like a sound coming from the bottom of a deep well. His eyelids fluttered as he struggled to open them, his vision blurring before it slowly started to clear.

The guard was a heavyset man, probably in his early fifties, with a kind face that set Christopher at ease, a comforting presence in the chaos. His uniform shirt was damp at the collar, and his badge slightly crooked. There was a steadiness in the way he worked; it suggested years of dealing with frightened kids. The steady stream of air from the mask was oddly soothing, filling his lungs with a refreshing coolness.

"Just try to relax and breathe normally," the guard

advised, his tone gentle but firm. "Your friend's banged up too, but he'll be all right. He took a nasty shot to the nose. He'll definitely be feeling it in the morning."

Christopher turned his head slowly, the motion draining what little strength he had left. He wanted to see Tommy, to make sure he was really okay. All he could make out at first were Tommy's feet, positioned awkwardly, like two halves of a mismatched pair. One sneaker was untied, and the other stained with blood. The soles were scuffed raw from the struggle. For some reason, the sight made Christopher think of a joke. *We're 69,* he thought, a small, private chuckle escaping him before it twisted into a cough that rattled his chest.

"Hey, kid, take it easy," the guard said, his voice full of concern. "I've got an ambulance on the way to check you both out. What's your name?"

"Christopher," he replied, weak and shaky. "What's yours?"

"McCormick, Richard McCormick. And no, you can't call me Dick."

Despite everything, Christopher laughed, though the effort brought on another round of coughing that left him gasping.

"Chris?" came a voice from nearby, one he recognized instantly. He sat up a little, wincing at the sharp ache in his lower back.

Tommy was sitting up too, their eyes meeting across the small distance between them. Relief washed over Christopher. Tommy was alive, though he looked like he'd been through hell. His nose was swollen and crooked, dried blood streaked beneath it, and his lip was split. He looked like a boy who'd just aged five years in a single afternoon.

"Damn, Tommy, you look like I feel," Christopher said.

"Is my nose still on my face?" He touched it gingerly, wincing at the swollen, misshapen flesh.

"Yeah, but it doesn't look much like a nose anymore. More like a pear, maybe even a funky piece of squash."

"Don't worry, Tommy," Richard interjected. "Doctors can work wonders these days. They'll fix your nose, probably better than before."

Tommy listened, grimacing. "That's cool, as long as they don't give me a small, skinny M.J. nose."

Richard frowned. "M.J. nose?"

"Michael Jackson," Tommy muttered, lying back with a sigh as if the explanation alone had drained him.

Richard chuckled, the sound breaking the tension.

"You had to ask," Christopher said, shaking his head slightly, though the motion made him dizzy. He tried to focus. "Hey, Tommy, what was that secret weapon you supposedly had in mind?"

Tommy let out a weak laugh. "Well, I had a can of mace, but it seems like I got maced by the ugly stick instead."

Christopher scoffed, but his thoughts were racing. The shock of what had happened was wearing off, replaced by a gnawing dread. He wondered what they had gotten themselves into.

The wail of sirens grew louder as the ambulance approached. Richard stood, his silhouette blotting out the bright yellow rim of the morning sun. The light caught on the sweat at his temple as he waved down the paramedics. The ambulance pulled into the lot with lights flashing. The world seemed to move in slow motion as the paramedics jumped out, their movements quick and efficient, a stark contrast to Christopher's sluggish haze.

"We need a plan," Christopher said quietly to Tommy.

"Definitely," Tommy murmured, though his eyes betrayed fear of what had happened, fear of what was coming.

As the paramedics reached them, Christopher felt a wave of exhaustion crash over him. The adrenaline was fading fast, leaving him weak and disoriented. A woman with kind eyes knelt beside him, gently checking his vitals.

"How ya feelin', slugger?" she asked.

"Tired."

"We're going to take good care of you. Just try to

relax."

He nodded, though the tension in his chest refused to ease. He could feel Tommy's gaze on him, and could sense the worry floating in the air. They had both been through something terrifying, something that had changed them, though neither of them understood it yet.

As the stretcher lifted him, Christopher closed his eyes, still hearing the murmur of paramedics.

The ride to St. Anthony's Memorial was uneventful; and the air was thick with silence. The vinyl bench was sticky against his skin, and the overhead light buzzed faintly while its glow pulsed in time with the siren's wail. Christopher felt the gentle rocking of the vehicle, and his mind circled back to Claudia, with those fierce eyes.

When the doors finally swung open, the bright hospital lights blinded him, and a sharp smell of antiseptic filled his lungs. He was wheeled through the sterile halls with the squeak of rubber soles on polished tile echoing like gunshots.

The intake was brief. Christopher's injuries amounted to a deep bruise across his lower back and a scraped arm. The blow had knocked the wind out of him, and the shock was enough to send him under for a moment, but nothing was broken. He was released within a couple of hours.

Tommy, however, needed more care. The doctor examined his broken nose, cleaned him up, and reset the bone with gauze packing to keep it in place. His face was swollen and tender, but it was nothing a few weeks of healing wouldn't fix.

Mr. and Mrs. Price arrived shortly after, their voices full of worry as they hovered over their son. Their presence was steady, though Christopher could sense the anger beneath their concern.

Detached from it all, Christopher called his mother for a ride. He wanted to go home. More than that, he needed space, needed to think. The necklace from his dream weighed heavily on his mind.

His mother's face was etched with worry when she arrived, but he assured her he was fine. They drove home in silence while the day's events hung between them.

When they pulled into the driveway, Christopher told her he wanted to take a nap. She hesitated but didn't press, understanding at least on some level that he needed to be alone, needed rest.

Upstairs, his room felt alien, as if it had been longing for him. The walls seemed to close in, the once comforting space now eerily quiet. None of it felt like his anymore, none of it except the necklace.

Moving with purpose, he went to the closet and pried up the loose boards he had hidden years before. The wood creaked as if reluctant to give up its secret. Dust curled in the air, catching the slant of afternoon light. The silver chain gleamed as though untouched by time. He picked it up, the weight familiar in his hand.

He slipped it over his head and felt an immediate surge of calm, a security so strong it settled into his bones. Nothing could hurt him now. And yet, along with the peace came sudden exhaustion. His vision blurred as he staggered toward the bed.

"I'll just lie here for a minute," he murmured, collapsing into the sheets.

The necklace rested against his chest, heavy and alive. It seemed to pulse once, faintly. Aware. His eyes fluttered shut, and he sank into darkness.

For Christopher, the dreams started immediately.

13

The light poured through the window, golden and soft. Drisana's hair spilled across her shoulders like a dark river. Her laughter echoed, too long, as if the air refused to let it fade.

Risto's hands brushed her cheek. "I love you." The words slipped from his mouth, but they didn't sound like his voice.

A boy's laughter now. Risto was smaller, legs pumping as he ran across a crowded marketplace. The air smelled of sweat and spices, voices colliding in a dozen directions. His mother's hand tugged him forward, her eyes searching the tree line.

The mountains loomed, tall and still, the sky too blue to be real. Then his father appeared, broad and smiling, arms outstretched. Risto leapt, weightless, straight into his father's chest.

Camile's joy glowed like a firelight. For a moment, the world stilled, their faces locked together in a perfect frame of love.

The frame blurred.

Risto again, but older now, with sweat on his brow, his hands steadying a fence post. The sharp smell of cut cedar filled the air, and dust floated in the sunlight like golden ash. The rhythm of his work stilled when Drisana stepped into view. She bent, picked up his hammer, and without a word began pounding it against the side of the house, striking the beams. Each thud landed sharp and jarring, too loud for the quiet day. Her movements were stiff, mechanical.

"Drisana?" Risto's voice wavered. He took a step toward her.

She didn't answer. The hammer fell again and again, the sound echoing inside his skull.

Slowly she turned, eyes blank, face drained of life. "That's enough," she said flatly. "Wake up."

* * *

Christopher's eyes slowly fluttered open. The ceiling fan above him whirred softly on its lowest setting, the gentle hum filling the room with a constant, droning sound. The blades cut through a shaft of evening sunlight leaking in through the blinds. He felt drained, as though all the energy had been sapped from his body. It was a struggle just to move.

As he lay there, disoriented, he became aware of a persistent knocking on his bedroom door. Each knock rattled the frame, small and impatient.

How long have I been lying here? he wondered, his thoughts sluggish and unfocused.

Slowly, he sat up, his movements stiff and unnatural, like a figure rising from a coffin. He shook his head, trying to clear the fog from his mind. The knocking at the door continued, insistent.

"Just a minute. I'm coming," Christopher called, his voice hoarse.

"What are you doing in there?" came Tommy's voice, tinged with impatience.

Relieved, Christopher swung his legs off the bed. Walking felt strange, as if he were gliding. He reached for the door but couldn't feel the knob beneath his hand. His hand tingled, feeling numb. Unease was rising in his gut.

The knob turned. Tommy stuck his head in, his nose draped in a bandage with splints. The voice that followed was a dull, nasal monotone. "Finally. I thought I'd be collecting social security before you answered. And what's with the jewelry? Starting a cult?"

"I'm having the weirdest sensation," Christopher muttered.

"Oh great, *and* you're high."

Christopher lifted the necklace over his head. The moment it cleared, a flood of sensation rushed through him, pins and needles, his whole body waking at once. He dropped the chain and staggered.

"Whoa, you all right?" Tommy grabbed his arm.

Christopher steadied himself, dazed. "Strange." He sank onto the bed, his head heavy.

Tommy eyed the necklace on the floor. "Strange, huh? I'm beat to hell and you're tripping off some shiny trinket. Where'd you get that?"

"That's a long story."

"Well, I've got time."

Christopher hesitated, then nodded. "It started when I was ten…"

Tommy groaned, "No, no, don't give me the saga."

"Sit down. You wanted to hear it," Christopher said.

Tommy sighed and sat down. "All right. Go on."

"It started when I was ten," Christopher repeated, recounting how he had found the necklace, the strange feelings that had followed, and how he had kept it hidden even from his mother. As he spoke, the memory sharpened, the sharp glint of metal half-buried in dirt, and the odd chill that had crawled over him the moment he touched it.

He told Tommy of the dream where he was a man in the countryside, building a fence. Then another one where he was a sheriff in a dusty town with an old man who left him unsettled, as though he were missing some vital connection.

Tommy listened closely now, his usual sarcasm fading into silence. The more Christopher spoke, the more questions tangled between them, each detail hinting at something larger, something neither of them could yet understand.

Their conversation stretched long into the night, the room darkening around them. The hum of the fan became a kind of metronome, counting off the hours. Christopher's story unfolded, the weight of the past and the unknown pressing in.

Eventually, Tommy stayed the night, both too wrapped up to part ways. But as the hours dragged on, Christopher lay awake, his mind racing with everything he'd shared. The necklace lay on the floor beside his bed. As he stared into the dark, listening to the house settle, he couldn't shake the feeling this was only the beginning. He believed that the dreams and the necklace were leading him toward something he couldn't yet see. And whatever it was, it was coming, whether he was ready or not.

14

Adriel carefully guided his horse through the dense forest, each step deliberate as he navigated the thick underbrush. The canopy overhead filtered the sunlight into scattered beams, casting shadows on the forest floor. His second horse, laden with the spoils of a successful hunt, two deer and a wild pig, followed closely behind, its hooves crunching softly on the fallen leaves. Though the thrill of the hunt always stirred something primal within him, his thoughts were fixed on home. His heart ached for the warmth of his wife and the laughter of his son. The sooner he saw their faces, the sooner he would feel at peace.

The rest of Adriel's hunting party wasn't far behind, but he had a habit of forging ahead whenever they neared the village. The anticipation of reuniting with his family always quickened his pace, as if the closer he got, the stronger the pull toward home became. He was a man deeply respected in the village, his strength tempered by survival. As a boy of ten, he had endured the horrors of World War III, losing both parents to the violence. Alone and terrified, he fled into the hills, emerging years later hardened but alive. The memory of smoke and gunfire still visited him at times, reminding him that peace was fragile, never promised. The earth itself had healed alongside him. The animals repopulated, and forests returned, until life could be built again from the ruins.

The trees began to thin. Patches of sunlight spilled through the branches, the air lighter, fresher. Adriel could hear faint music drifting on the breeze. He smiled at the sound, heart lifting. *It's the villagers… my friends, my family. Oh, Camile, Risto, how I long to see your faces.*

He stepped from the tree line, pausing to take in the open grasslands bathed in afternoon light. A crowd moved and mingled across the clearing, laughter and voices carrying. Adriel inhaled deeply, savoring the sight, then urged his horses forward.

* * *

"Mom, I don't see Dad yet. When's he going to get here?" Risto asked, his voice impatient as he scanned the trees.

"You must be patient, Risto. Your father will be here

soon," Camile reassured him, resting a hand on his shoulder. Her eyes never left the forest's edge.

Just then, music swelled through the air, a lively tune from the village band. "Mom, let's go watch the players," Risto said, tugging her arm.

Camile hesitated, glancing between her son and the forest. "If we watch the band, we might miss your father when he comes out of the woods."

A voice rang out from the crowd: "They're back! They're back!" Heads turned toward the trees.

Camile's heart leapt. She scooped Risto into her arms despite his protests.

"Mom, what are you doing?" he exclaimed, clutching her shoulders.

"Look, Risto, your father's back!" Her voice shook with emotion as she hurried toward the tree line.

Adriel stood there, strong and steady, sunlight behind him. When his eyes found them, his chest swelled. He watched Camile run, their son twisting in her arms to get a better look. The sight of them both flooded him with peace. The long days in the forest, the blood on his hands, the silence of the hunt, none of it mattered now.

Risto wriggled free and sprinted the last steps, his laughter bubbling. Adriel knelt, catching him, lifting him high.

When Camile reached them, she threw her arms

around Adriel, holding him tight. For a moment, the world disappeared.

Risto, meanwhile, was already circling the horse, marveling at the deer and the great wild pig. To him, they were more than food, they were proof of the courage and skill he dreamed of one day claiming for himself. He touched the coarse hair of the pig, his small hand hesitant, as though it might still wake and challenge him.

He glanced back at his parents, still lost in each other, his mother's fingers brushing his father's jaw, his father's gaze warm with love. All felt right in the world.

Unable to wait any longer, Risto tugged at Adriel's shirt.

"Pardon me, darling," Adriel said with a chuckle, turning. "I sense a critter among us."

"What's that look for?" he asked, bending to eye level with his son.

"I was just wondering if you two were finished yet."

"Well, I believe we are. What's on your mind?"

"Food and the party!" Risto laughed.

Every year, after the hunters returned, the villagers gathered for a celebration, a feast to honor the hunters and remember the war's end. Torches were already being lit around the square, their smoke curling into the evening. The sound of drums carried faintly, steady as a heartbeat. This year felt even more special, a marker of how far they had come.

The other men emerged from the forest, voices carrying.

"Well, it sounds like everyone made it back. What do you say we head to the party now, huh?" Adriel said, ruffling Risto's hair.

"Yeah! Can I lead your horse, Dad?"

"Sure."

Adriel handed him the reins, watching with pride as the boy gripped them tight. With his other arm, he pulled Camile close, and together they walked toward the village. The sun dipped lower, casting a golden glow, laughter and music swelling ahead.

The celebration burst to life under the evening sky. Tables groaned beneath roasted meats, fresh bread, and hearty stews. The aromas mingled with the sweetness of wildflowers scattered across the tables. Music soared, while couples danced, spinning and twirling in the open clearing. Children squealed with delight as lambs and baby goats were brought among them, their hands reaching to pet soft coats. They waited eagerly for the sack of wooden toys, prizes crafted by the villagers and treasured more than gold.

Adriel and Camile danced together, their movements graceful, effortless, as if the world itself had been made for their love. Risto watched them from the side, his chest swelling with pride. The firelight painted their faces in copper and gold, and he thought they looked like figures from one of the old legends.

At the edge of the gathering, a woman sat alone at a small table, robes flowing, jewelry glinting in the firelight. Her dark eyes scanned the crowd, always returning to Risto.

"Orenda," someone whispered behind him. "The fortune teller."

Risto shivered. The villagers said many things about her, maker of charms, teller of fates, maybe even a witch. Her bracelets clinked softly when she lifted her cup, but her gaze never wavered. It was the look of someone who knew too much, and wanted him to know it. He didn't care about the rumors; what unsettled him was that her gaze was fixed on him.

He turned away quickly, forcing himself to focus on the music, on the warmth of his family and the joy of the night. Whatever unease Orenda brought, he was determined not to let it spoil the celebration.

15

Christopher woke the next morning feeling more rested than he had expected. He and Tommy had talked late into the night, the weight of their conversation pressing on him long after the room had gone quiet. Sleep hadn't come easy, but when it finally did, it was deep and dreamless. For the first time in what felt like forever, he couldn't recall a single image or vision. For a moment, he lay still, savoring the quiet that filled his room as he tried to gather his thoughts.

The sound of steady breathing from nearby reassured him that Tommy was still fast asleep. Christopher recognized that rhythmic sound; it was too natural to be faked. A small chuckle escaped him as he imagined Darth Vader lying on the floor beside his bed. It was ridiculous, but comforting too, proof that some things could still feel ordinary.

Rolling over in his twin bed, Christopher turned to look at Tommy, who was sprawled out on the floor in an old military sleeping bag. The sight was almost comical. Tommy looked like a giant green bean with a face, his hair sticking up in all directions, and a small pool of drool already forming on his pillow. The faint sour-sleep smell clung to the bag, a reminder that boys weren't meant to live polished lives. Christopher couldn't help but wish he had a camera to capture the moment.

He stifled his laughter, not wanting to wake Tommy, but then something strange happened. In an instant, Tommy's head seemed to shift, to transform. Another person's head began to emerge from his, as if a second face were materializing from within. The apparition was light gray, ghostly, almost transparent, but unmistakable.

He drew in a sharp breath, and his heart pounded as he stared in disbelief. The new face turned slowly and locked eyes with him. The face was Claudia, but an older version, and she had a devilish grin that was unnerving. Her eyes were black slits with no distinct pupil, solid. His chest went cold, like ice water had poured through his ribs. Instinctively, his hand flew to his mouth, suppressing the scream that threatened to burst out.

They stared at each other for what felt like an eternity, until suddenly, the head leaned closer and whispered in a voice that seemed to echo from the depths of a nightmare.

"I'm always watching you."

The vision vanished as quickly as it had appeared, leaving Christopher trembling. He couldn't contain it any longer. He let out a shout, the sound tearing through the morning silence.

Tommy jolted awake, his eyes wide with confusion.

"Why are you screaming?" he asked groggily, rubbing the sleep from his face, still half-asleep and bewildered.

Christopher was now sitting upright in bed with his knees drawn to his chest, staring blankly ahead. His voice was hollow, almost robotic, as he whispered, "I saw souls. I saw *a* soul, *her* soul."

"What are you talking about?" Tommy asked, still confused.

Christopher turned to face him, his eyes wide and filled with a terror that Tommy had never seen before.

"No, I'm serious. I saw her soul. She spoke to me. She told me she was always watching me."

Tommy stared at him, the words slowly sinking in as he tried to make sense of what Christopher was saying. He pushed himself out of the sleeping bag and stood up, feeling the cool air against his skin as he tried to regain his bearings.

Christopher kept his eyes fixed on Tommy, half-expecting the ghostly vision to return, wondering if, somehow, Tommy was possessed and didn't even know it. The thought hit him hard, an image of Claudia riding beneath Tommy's skin like a shadow that could wear him as a mask. The thought was unsettling, sending a shiver down his spine, but it passed quickly.

"Okay, whose soul did you see? Was this another dream?" Tommy asked, still piecing things together.

"I don't know who she was, but she looked like Claudia, but older," Christopher said, his voice shaky. "But it wasn't a dream."

There was a long pause as Tommy processed the information, and Christopher watched him intently, as if expecting something terrible to happen.

"I was watching you sleep." Christopher pointed to the floor where Tommy's sleeping bag was. "I mean, I was awake, laughing at how you looked. It's not funny now, but it was then. Then I saw someone else's head come out of yours—*her* head."

Tommy looked around the room, his eyes searching for any sign of the supernatural. He glanced at the mirror behind him, half-expecting to see something unusual reflected back at him. Only his own battered reflection looked back, pale and irritated.

"Like a ghost," Christopher continued, his voice barely above a whisper. "And she said, 'I'm watching you,' or 'always watching you,' or something like that."

Tommy stared at his reflection, bewildered by the idea that something might have come out of his head. He patted his hair down, as if trying to smooth it or maybe to check for any lingering presence that Christopher had seen.

Christopher finally snapped out of his trance and swung his legs over the edge of the bed, standing up. "Man, Tommy, I have to figure this out."

Tommy, still reeling from the bizarre story, started to roll up his sleeping bag. "Maybe it *was* Claudia. Why don't we try to find her again, but in a different setting? No more mall scenes, though."

Christopher nodded, his thoughts racing. "You're right. Okay, but one weird look from Queen Psycho, and I'm out of there. Where do you think we should look first?"

Tommy paused, folding the sleeping bag neatly. "That's the other reason I came by last night, but I forgot to mention it. There's a party tonight at the park."

"The park?" Christopher questioned, his voice tinged with apprehension.

The park was the epicenter of social life for people their age. It was massive, spanning nearly five hundred yards in length and width, dotted with trees and winding paths. It was where the toughest guys and the prettiest girls gathered, along with the usual mix of alcohol, sex, drugs, and rock 'n' roll. Every weekend, the park was packed, and Christopher could already picture the bonfires glowing through the trees, and the smell of cheap beer. Then there was the way the crowd always teetered on the edge of violence. And by the time he and Tommy would arrive, it would be at its peak, the most dangerous.

His heart sank at the thought. The park was a place where things could spiral out of control quickly, where the line between fun and danger blurred.

"I don't know, Tommy. The park isn't exactly what I had in mind considering what happened at the mall."

"Look, I know the park can get wild, but if Claudia's going to be anywhere, it'll be there. Plus, we stick together, and we'll be fine. We just need to keep our heads on straight and not do anything stupid."

Christopher hesitated, the memory of the ghostly visage still fresh in his mind. But he knew Tommy was right. If they were going to find Claudia again, the park was their best bet.

"All right, but let's be careful. I don't want to end up like last time."

Tommy nodded. "Agreed. We'll go in, find her, and get out. No unnecessary risks."

As they prepared for the day ahead, the tension in the room was palpable. Both boys knew that by nightfall everything could change, and the weight of that realization hung heavy in the air. They went about their routines in silence, each lost in their own thoughts, bracing for what the hours ahead might bring.

By the time they were ready to leave, the sun had fully risen. Christopher glanced out the window, watching neighbors start their morning as if nothing were amiss. He felt a strange sense of foreboding, as if the ordinary rhythm of the day was only a mask, hiding something waiting just out of sight.

Tommy broke the silence, his voice cutting through the weight that pressed between them. "Let's do this."

Christopher nodded, grabbing his jacket from the back of a chair. As they stepped out the door, he couldn't help but think that whatever they were walking into had already begun, and neither of them had a choice but to follow it to the end.

16

Years passed, and Risto grew into a man, his life shaped by the trials and joys that had marked his journey. He married a beautiful woman named Drisana, and together they built a life on the outskirts of Hope, the village where Risto had spent most of his years. Hope was more than just a place to him; it was a sanctuary, the first place where he had found peace after a childhood marked by loss and turmoil.

His parents had passed during his teenage years, a time that had marked a profound turning point in his life. His father, Adriel, had died on a hunting trip, the victim of what the villagers believed to be a grizzly bear attack. The men who had been with him never saw the bear, but the remains found in the mountains that day left little room for doubt. The story of that hunt was retold for years, in half-whispers by the fire, always with a glance toward Risto as if his silence could confirm or deny the truth. The tragedy had shattered Risto, and not long after, his mother, Camile, succumbed to grief. She had refused food and water, retreating into herself after Adriel's death until she wasted away. When she passed, it was said that even a child could have lifted her frail body off the bed.

Despite these heartbreaking losses, Risto was not left entirely alone. Orenda, a woman both feared and respected in the village, took him under her wing. She became his teacher, mentor, and in many ways, a godmother. Orenda was no ordinary villager; her knowledge reached into the deeper, more mysterious arts of prophecy and magic. The scent of incense clung to her clothes, her cottage always crowded with flickering candles. Under her guidance, Risto gradually earned the respect of the villagers, who began to see him as a leader. Yet, despite the outward calm of his life, there was always an undercurrent of unease, particularly when he met Orenda's watchful eyes. Something in her gaze always lingered too long, as if she were reading not just his face but the marrow of him.

One evening, Risto and Drisana prepared to attend the annual hunter's party, a celebration that had been a painful reminder of his father's death in previous years. For a long time, Risto had avoided the event, unable to face the memories it stirred. But this year felt different. He felt ready, stronger, more in control of his emotions. Walking hand in hand with Drisana, they left their home, the comfort of their love a steady presence between them. The moonlight touched her cheek as they walked, and her smile steadied him. They made small talk as they walked, and every so often, their eyes would meet, a reminder of their deep love.

As they neared the village, the sounds of laughter and music reached their ears, growing louder with each step. The glow of torches illuminated the path ahead, the celebration in full swing with villagers dancing and enjoying the festivities. The air carried the scents of spiced meat roasting on spits, and ale splashing from mugs. The sound of fiddles rose above the chatter, carrying the rhythm of joy. The sight of the joyful crowd filled Risto with a mix of anticipation and nostalgia.

Upon entering the village, they were quickly swept apart by their friends. Daniel, one of Risto's oldest and dearest friends, appeared out of the crowd and grabbed him, pulling him away to have a drink with him and a girl he had just met. Daniel was already well on his way to drunkenness, his speech slurred and his steps unsteady. He was eager to show off his latest conquest, though Risto knew from experience that Daniel's taste in women, especially after a few drinks, was questionable at best.

"You know, I've met the puurfect girl," Daniel slurred, his words running together as he swayed on his feet.

"Have you?" Risto replied, a hint of amusement in his voice. "I bet she's beautiful too. At least she's beautiful to you right now, my friend."

Daniel stopped abruptly, causing Risto to brace himself, half-expecting his friend to topple over. Instead, Daniel turned his bleary eyes to him. "I think you just insulted me."

"You think I just insulted you?"

"Yeah!" Daniel confirmed, punctuating his response with a small, unsteady burp.

"Well, I did! Old friend, you tend to find beautiful women only after several drinks in the evening."

Daniel blinked at him, his expression a mix of confusion and wounded pride. "I love you, brother. But she is, she's beautiful," he insisted as he resumed dragging Risto through the crowd, his grip on his arm firm despite his inebriated state.

Before they could reach Daniel's new love interest, they found their path blocked by Orenda.

She stood before them, her eyes locking onto Risto with an intensity that made him pause. Her robes caught the torchlight, shimmering faintly as if they held their own glow.

"Good evening, Risto. What's wrong with him?" Orenda asked, her gaze flicking over Daniel with a mixture of disdain and curiosity.

Daniel glared back, clearly not appreciating the interruption. "Come on, Risto," he urged, tugging on his shirt as if to pull him away from Orenda's scrutiny.

"Daniel is taking me to meet his date for the evening."

Orenda gave Daniel a dismissive look before turning her full attention back to Risto. "I need to speak with you in private."

"Ooooh," Daniel drawled, his voice dripping with drunken mischief.

Risto stifled a laugh at his friend's antics. "Can it wait until tomorrow? I'd like to just relax tonight."

"I'm sorry, Risto. It concerns your father," she replied, her voice softening just enough to convey the gravity of her words.

Even in his drunken state, Daniel straightened up at the mention of Adriel's name. "Hey, Risto, if you need to be alone…"

"No," Risto interrupted. He turned back to Orenda, his expression more serious. "Can we meet in half an hour?"

Orenda's eyes narrowed slightly as she glanced at Daniel, disapproving. But after a moment, she nodded. "Yes, that's fine. Meet me at my home."

Risto nodded, his thoughts already drifting away from the festivities.

As he allowed Daniel to continue leading him through

the crowd, his mind was no longer on the party or the girl Daniel was so eager to introduce him to. Instead, it was filled with memories of Adriel, the man who had been his hero—his anchor.

Daniel continued to brag about his mysterious beauty, but Risto's responses were automatic. He couldn't shake the feeling of unease that had settled in the pit of his stomach. What could Orenda possibly have to say about Adriel after all these years? Whatever it was, it couldn't be good. Orenda was not one to bring up the past lightly. The weight of that name, Adriel, pressed deep on his heart, calling back the sound of his voice, and the steady presence of his father that had once made the world feel safe.

17

After spending some time with Daniel and his date, Risto found the right moment to slip away. He knew Daniel would not mind; in fact, he probably would not remember much by morning anyway.

Orenda lived on the outskirts, farthest from the rest of the villagers, a subtle acknowledgment that she was not particularly well liked, and perhaps that she preferred solitude.

The night was calm, the stars shining brightly overhead, and the only sound accompanying Risto was the crunch of dirt and dried leaves underfoot. A thin stream of smoke from the village drifted through the treetops; the music behind him rose and fell like surf. As he walked, he occasionally paused to ensure the celebration was still ongoing. He had left Daniel leaning against a tree, chatting animatedly with his girlfriend, the rest of the world forgotten.

"Hey, stranger," a voice called out suddenly, snapping Risto out of his thoughts. He spun around, muscles tensing, ready to defend himself if necessary.

"Whoa, it's okay. It's me," Drisana said, stepping into the moonlight with a playful smile. Her hair caught the starlight; her breath smelled faintly of apple wine. The relief that hit him was sharp enough to sting.

Risto exhaled, his heart still racing. "What are you doing here?" he asked, trying to steady his breathing.

She stepped closer, her hand gently brushing against his cheek. "I heard that Orenda had asked for you. She's such a pain, don't you think?"

"She can be," he admitted, his tension easing slightly. "So... what are you doing out here?"

"I was just feeling playful. Thought you might want to sneak into the woods with me before meeting the beast." She leaned in and kissed him deeply, her arms wrapping around him.

Risto melted into the kiss, heat unfurling in his chest as the weight on his shoulders eased. His love for her drowned out everything else.

She took his hand, leading him further into the dark woods. The leaves whispered under their boots; somewhere a nighthawk trilled and fell quiet, as if it, too, were watching.

As their passion ignited, Risto could not shake the feeling that something was off. The ground beneath them was uncomfortable, but that was not the source of his unease. A thread of cold slid down his spine, instinct, not weather. He became aware of footsteps approaching, someone moving purposefully through the woods. His senses flared, warning him that the intruder knew exactly where to find them.

"Drisana, someone's coming. Stay still," he whispered.

He hoped whoever it was would pass by without noticing them, but the figure continued to approach, a silhouette against the moonlight, stopping just a few feet away.

"Who's there?" Risto demanded.

The figure was a woman, but in the dim light, he could not make out who it was.

"Risto? Is that you?" The woman's voice was familiar, and as she pushed through the branches into the moonlight, her face became clear.

"Oh my God! What are you doing? What have you done to me?!" she screamed, her voice filled with horror, before running away in tears.

Risto's heart plummeted as he stared at her in disbelief. It was Drisana. *But if Drisana is standing there, then who am I with?* He thought.

He turned to look at his partner, dread pooling in his stomach.

Orenda's eyes met his, her expression a twisted mix of amusement and malice. She still held him close, as if they were lovers.

"Let go of me!" Risto shouted, yanking himself away from her.

She held him tight, still smiling maliciously.

"I said let go!"

"Wait!"

"Let go of me, woman!" Risto struggled to his feet, panic clawing at his chest. He was about to run after Drisana when Orenda's grip tightened on his arm, her strength surprising him.

"Wait, you fool!" she commanded, swinging him back around to face her. "If you don't want to lose her forever, you must listen to me now."

Risto's eyes were wide with fear and confusion, but he forced himself to listen, desperate to fix whatever had just happened.

"Now, hold my hand and repeat after me," Orenda ordered, her voice firm and unyielding.

"What? We're wasting time! I need to..."

"You must listen to me! Now do it!" she barked, her tone leaving no room for argument.

Feeling cornered with no other option, Risto grabbed

Orenda's hand and stared into her eyes, trying to muster some semblance of trust in her.

"Repeat after me," she said.

She led him through a series of strange, rhythmic chants. The words felt ancient, foreign, but Risto focused on getting the pronunciation right, terrified of what might happen if he messed up. The syllables stuck to his tongue. When she finally stopped, Risto opened his eyes, anxiety and disorientation clouding his thoughts.

"Now what?" he asked, his heart pounding as he scanned the area for any sign of Drisana.

"Shhh… stop," Orenda whispered, placing a finger on his lips. "Listen to me. Come with me into the clearing, where we'll talk and wait."

"Wait for what?" Risto asked, his frustration mounting.

"For Drisana, of course."

"What do you mean? You're not making any sense."

"My child, have I ever led you astray?"

Risto's eyes answered that question, but she ignored it.

"Just remember, stay calm, and don't speak unless spoken to."

They walked to the clearing together, the night air cool against Risto's skin. The hunters' party carried on in the distance, laughter and music a stark contrast to the turmoil inside him. Shame and anger mixed bitterly in his chest.

He kept looking at Orenda—nervous. He was unable to reconcile what had just happened. *How had I been so easily deceived? And what have I done to Drisana?* He thought.

Orenda stood in silence and smiled, as if everything were perfectly normal.

Suddenly, Risto heard footsteps approaching. He tensed, turning toward the sound, every muscle in his body coiled with anticipation. A woman stepped into the moonlight, and relief flooded through him as he recognized her. It was Drisana, her eyes meeting him with a warm smile. No fury, no accusation, only the softness of recognition.

"Hello, you two. What are you up to?" she asked, her tone light and cheerful.

"I was just telling Risto about a new project I'm working on," Orenda replied smoothly.

Drisana turned to Risto, noticing the pallor of his face. "Are you okay? You look like you've seen a ghost," she said, touching his cheek.

Risto could hardly believe what was happening. She did not remember anything. It was as if none of it had occurred. The chant had done more than cool the air; it had rewritten it.

"Hello? Are you okay?" Drisana repeated, waving her fingers in front of his face.

"Yes," Risto forced himself to respond, though his

voice wavered. "I'm fine. Actually, I just got here before you did. I haven't heard much yet."

"Well, I just thought I'd say hello. Orenda mentioned you'd be here and asked me to stop by," she explained.

Risto looked at Orenda, stunned by the seamlessness of her deception. She simply gave him an approving nod, her expression inscrutable. He understood the nod for what it was: *I can take it all away, and I can give it back.*

"Well, I'll leave you two to your business. I'm going back to the party, some of my friends are getting a bit wild," Drisana said, leaning in to kiss Risto on the cheek before leaving.

"Goodnight, Orenda."

"Goodnight."

Risto watched in disbelief as Drisana walked away, her steps light and carefree.

Orenda, observing his reaction with satisfaction, asked, "Are you going to be okay?"

Risto stared off into the distance, his mind reeling from the night's events. "I'll be fine. This may take some getting used to, but I'll be fine," he said, though his voice lacked conviction. He flexed his hands once, twice, as if confirming they were still his.

"Well, before you dwell on this too long, you should come inside. I'll explain why I asked you here in the first place," she said.

Risto, still in shock, realized his thoughts were jumbled, and a strange thirst gnawed at him. "Do you have any water?"

"Travel does that," she said. "To me, it brings sleep. To you, thirst."

He froze at her choice of words. *Travel.* The kind that bent time. He didn't want to ask how many times she had done it, or what else she could change.

She turned toward the door, "Come inside. There's more you need to hear."

He followed, the thirst gnawing deeper with every step. Behind them, the clearing filled again with the hum of crickets and faint music, but none of it sounded real anymore.

18

Once inside Orenda's house, Risto was struck by the disarray. He had seen it before, growing up, but it never ceased to amaze him how untidy the place was. Books were scattered everywhere, mostly on spells and magic, and cobwebs clung to every surface. The air carried a musk of damp parchment, and something acrid that made the back of his throat itch. The cups on the table were coated in dust and cobwebs. Bundles of dried plants dangled from the rafters, their shadows bending across the walls like skeletal hands.

Orenda lit a candle, casting a low, mysterious glow over the room. The flame danced, casting a weak circle of light pooling in a house that seemed determined to remain half in darkness.

"Please, Risto. Sit," she said.

Risto had become irritated after what had happened and remained standing. "Look, Orenda, I came here thinking about my father, but then I ended up in the bushes with you, thinking you were Drisana. Now, somehow, everything's back to normal."

Orenda continued to arrange a few more candles, her face serene, almost amused by Risto's frustration. Her composure was infuriating; the corners of her mouth twitched as though she were savoring a private joke.

"I'm glad to see you're having such a wonderful time with all of this."

"Please, Risto," she repeated, "sit down, and I will open your eyes."

He hesitated, then threw up his hands in frustration before reluctantly sitting down, cross-legged at the edge of a pit that was cut out of the floor in the center of the room. Ash lined the basin, thick with years of old burnings and unidentifiable remnants. He watched Orenda move around the pit, her gaze distant as if she were lost in thought.

"How old are you, Risto?"

The question caught him off guard. "What does that have to do with anything?"

"Just answer."

"Thirty-five," he said flatly.

She paused, her eyes softening in a rare flicker of

empathy. "The same age your father was when he died. I've waited a long time to tell you what I know, longer than you realize. Now the time has come."

She continued moving with deliberate purpose as she gathered powders and herbs, then pointed at the necklace hanging around his neck.

"That necklace, who gave it to you?"

He glanced down, fingering the crystal that hung from the chain.

"My mother gave it to me on her deathbed. She said my father had it put away for me."

Orenda nodded, as if confirming something to herself, then sat at the edge of the pit, opposite Risto.

"What I'm about to tell you won't be easy," she explained. "After your mother died, I took you under my wing. Do you remember?"

"Yes, I remember." His voice was softer now, wary of where this was going.

"All those years were preparation."

"Prepared for what?"

She raised a closed fist above her head. "For what you're about to see."

She threw what looked like a stone into the pit. Instantly, a large, cylindrical flame erupted, about five feet tall and three feet in diameter. It was solid blue in color, yet transparent. Risto could still see Orenda sitting across from him. The light painted her face ghostly, her features stretched and shifting as if her skin barely belonged to her.

Startled, Risto instinctively shifted to one knee, ready to flee. He looked to Orenda for reassurance, and she calmly motioned for him to sit back down. As he did, the flame began to subside, collapsing inward until it formed what looked like a window into the night sky. Risto stared, entranced by the sight of stars and electric blue clouds. The depth of it pulled at him like vertigo, as though he might topple forward and fall into this other place.

"You've got my attention," he said.

Orenda spoke softly, "Risto, what you're looking at is a time window. You can go anywhere you want."

"Wait," he said, holding up one hand. "Are you talking about time travel?"

"Yes."

His eyes dropped back to the window, his mind racing as he tried to comprehend what he was seeing. Orenda moved closer, sitting beside him as she explained.

"I waited to tell you until I felt like you were ready."

"Can I touch it?" he asked, his voice trembling with a mix of fear and curiosity.

"Yes."

As Risto's fingers touched the edge of the window, a strange sensation washed over him. Cold first, then nothing. A rush of emptiness, like every nerve had been erased. He could not feel his body anymore, as if he were weightless. Gasping, he pushed his hand deeper into the window, only to find that his hand had vanished. All he could see was his wrist, with nothing attached.

"My God, what's happening?" he said. His eyes were wide with fear and excitement, continuing to stare at the empty space where his hand should have been.

"Your hand is now somewhere else. It's either in the past, the future, or a different moment. If you leave it there long enough, you'll feel the draw."

"The draw? What's that?"

"Time will start to remake you," she said. "It won't kill you, but without an anchor, it will pull you apart and rebuild you in another place, another life. You'll forget who you were. That's why the necklace matters."

Risto felt a force tugging at him, like gravity was pulling him deeper. The pull was steady, patient, like a tide, promising to pull you in.

"No," he whispered, and with little effort, he leaned back, pulling his hand free. He turned it over, relieved to see it intact, wiggling his fingers in front of his face. The sensation of weightlessness faded, and he felt his body return to normal.

"How do you feel?" Orenda asked.

He took a deep breath, lowering his hand. "Strangely, I feel fine. It's odd, but I do feel okay." He sat back down and crossed his legs.

"So, now that I know about the time window, what does this have to do with my father?"

19

As Orenda began to speak, her voice was heavy with reluctance. "I've dreaded this moment for a long time," she admitted. "There's no easy way to tell you this, Risto, so I'll be blunt. You might get angry, and you'll probably want to deny everything I'm about to say. But I need you to remember one thing: why would I lie about something like this after everything I've shown you?"

Risto's heart pounded as he listened, sensing the gravity of her words. The room felt smaller, the candlelight tightening into a jaundiced ring around the two of them.

"Risto, your father is not dead."

Risto's face tightened in disbelief. He replayed her words in his mind, uncertain if he had heard her correctly. "I'm sorry, Orenda. Did you just say my father is not dead?"

Orenda's serious expression didn't waver. She was not joking, and the weight of her revelation left Risto at a loss for words.

"Orenda, it's late. We're both tired, and you've already shown me a lot tonight," he began, trying to escape the conversation. He got up, a reflex born of old wounds, leaving before the hurt lands.

But she wouldn't let him off the hook. She followed him as he walked. "Don't act like you can just walk away from this, Risto," she said firmly. "Your father stepped into a time window just like the one you saw tonight."

Risto tried to process what she was saying. A pulse throbbed in his temple, and the word *window* became a blade. "No, my father was on a hunting trip, surrounded by people. He wasn't anywhere near a time window."

"That's where you're wrong," she countered. "A window can be created wherever it's convenient. And, if I recall correctly, your father went missing, didn't he?"

He looked away, memories flooding back. "Yes, he did," he admitted, feeling a flicker of doubt, and remembering the details: the hillside, the men's stunned faces, the torn saddle, and fragments that had never fit quite right.

Orenda pressed on. "Exactly. He went missing, and everyone assumed he was attacked by a bear. But, Risto, he didn't just disappear, he was pulled through time."

Risto shook his head, trying to dismiss the growing suspicion. "This is crazy. He was lost in the woods, and before anyone could find him, a bear attacked him. It's tragic, but he didn't jump through time."

Orenda's tone softened. "Maybe you're right. Maybe I'm just jumping to conclusions. But isn't it strange that a skilled hunter like your father would get lost in the woods he knew so well?"

The seed of doubt took root in his mind. She had a point. His father had been an exceptional hunter, and the idea that he would get lost in familiar territory seemed unlikely. Adriel could read a trail like a map; even the trees had seemed to bend toward him.

"And even if he wasn't lost, it's still possible he was attacked by a bear, right?" she continued. "But isn't it odd that the last bear sighting in this area was long before you were born? Do you actually know what a bear looks like?"

Risto was caught off guard by the question. "Well, yeah, they have big claws and..." he started, but his description faltered. "You know, they're huge." Reluctantly, he admitted, "No."

She nodded. "Exactly. We can discuss carnivorous creatures another time, but for now, let's focus on your father."

Risto was frustrated. Heat rose in his chest; the urge to argue wrestled with the urge to believe. "Listen, Orenda, they found a body. It was next to my father's horse and his hunting gear. They even found this necklace," he said, clutching the crystal around his neck. "No one else had one like it."

"I agree," she said. "They found a body, but whose body was it?"

Risto was unconvinced. "You're saying someone else was with him? My father got sidetracked, and before he could find his way, he was attacked by something, maybe not a bear, but something."

She walked closer to him, her voice calm yet insistent. "I think your father was experimenting with the time window. During the process, someone attacked him. They struggled, and your father either killed the other person or wounded them badly. In his last act of defense, that person pushed your father into the window. Now your father is missing, and we have a dead body."

Risto stared at her. "How do you know it wasn't his body? Wouldn't someone have recognized him?"

Orenda's gaze was steady.

"Don't you remember? The body was unrecognizable. The assumption was that a bear or some other animal had mauled it. But I saw the body, and it wasn't your father's."

"How could you be so sure?" he demanded.

"Because the body had a scar between the thumb and index finger on the left hand. Your father didn't have that scar. I know because I gave that scar to a thief I once knew," she explained. Her eyes drifted as she spoke, chasing a ghost of memory.

Risto felt the weight of her words pressing down on him. This was too much. He walked around the room, rubbing his eyes, wondering, almost hoping, this was all a nightmare.

"I'm tired, Orenda. I'm tired of the games and the questions. Just tell me what's going on," he pleaded, standing in front of her, desperate for answers.

Her demeanor shifted, becoming more direct. She raised her chin. "I sent for him."

Risto's eyes narrowed. "What do you mean?"

"I told him I wanted the necklace. I explained that he wasn't the right person to control such power and that someone with more experience should study it."

"More experience? Sounds like jealousy to me. What does this necklace do that makes you want it so badly?"

She turned away, gathering her thoughts before facing him again. "It's a doorway to time itself. And it only answers your bloodline. The words are simple: *show me*. By itself, it reopens the last doorway used. Add a year, and it takes you there. Say *show me home*, and it drags you back to your rightful time. That's why your father could wield it, and why I cannot."

Risto looked down at the crystal around his neck,

realizing its significance. It was like the crystals she had used to create the time window in the pit, but this one was clear with a blue core. Cold bled from it into his palm.

"He thought he could control the universe," she said bitterly.

"My father wasn't reckless. He was logical, honest, and never one to chase fame or power," Risto argued. "You're not telling me everything. Start by explaining how it works since he's not here to do it."

Orenda sighed, clearly frustrated. She walked up to him, grabbing the crystal around his neck. "You hold it in your fist, speak the words, and the doorway answers. That's how it works."

Risto grabbed her wrist, shaking her loose. "That simple, huh?" he said, taking the necklace off, then holding it out to her. "If you want it so badly, take it."

Orenda was dumbfounded. She didn't move, didn't blink. She just stared at the necklace with fear written across her face.

Risto understood now. "Wait a minute," he said, lowering his hand. "You can't work it, can you? You just said bloodline controls it."

Her silence confirmed his suspicion.

"The most powerful woman I know can't control this piece of jewelry," he said, laughing. "It's all starting to make sense now. You wanted it so badly my father must've escaped you. Nothing else explains why he'd walk away. You must have really pissed him off."

He stepped closer, nearly nose to nose with her. The candle hissed between them. "Why don't we go ask him?"

Orenda's fear was unmistakable. She tried to back away, but Risto grabbed her shoulder, holding her in place.

"What are you afraid of? Tell me where he went. What doorway did he open?"

Orenda fumbled, looking away.

Risto tightened his grip, shaking her. "What doorway?"

"Like I said, the last one he used. If you speak the words now, it will take you to him."

Risto took a step back and placed the necklace back over his head. He grabbed Orenda again, pulling her to the center of the room. "You're coming with me."

"Where?"

"To find Adriel, to find my father. Then we'll find out what the hell is going on," he said, gripping the crystal tightly in his fist. Resolve settled over him like armor.

"I'm not going with you, you fool!" she protested, still struggling to twist free.

"Yes you are," he said, then reached behind his back and drew a large knife. He held the blade in one hand and the crystal in the other, pressing the steel close to her throat. His voice was cold and steady. "You're going whether you like it or not, understood?"

A whimper escaped her lips as Risto pulled her tight. He clenched the stone in his fist and spoke the words.

"Show me."

Stars burst into being around them, drifting in silence. At first they floated slow and scattered, then quickened, accelerating into a spiral. The points of light converged, swelling into a sphere ten feet across before settling into stillness. White filled the room. Loose pages lifted from the tables; dust spilled from the rafters in glowing veils.

They stood before the disc of light, its presence overwhelming.

He released her. Together they stared, awestruck. The light hovered, solid and calm, its surface rippled once, like a vast lung drawing breath on the other side.

20

Risto cautiously approached the disc, trying to see what lay beyond it. The air rippled like heat, making the hair on his arms stand on end. A low hum pulsed from the disc, like the whisper of a seashell pressed to his ear.

Orenda stood beside him, equally mesmerized. Her eyes reflected the glow, as though it were the altar she had waited her whole life to kneel before.

Suddenly, Risto grabbed her wrist. "Let's go!"

She shrieked, scratching and hitting him. "No! Let go of me!"

Though he didn't raise the knife, Risto took the blows and dragged her closer. In his haste he stumbled, losing his grip on both her wrist and the blade. The knife clattered to the floor. Orenda seized her chance and shoved him hard.

He went down, one boot sliding into the light. His

fingernails clawed at the dirt, desperate for a grip that wasn't there. The pull began, stronger than he'd imagined. It dragged at him with the hunger of a storm, sucking him in all the way to his shoulders. He clawed furrows in the floor, but the earth gave him nothing.

A hand seized his wrist—Orenda. She loomed above him, lips curling into a triumphant smile, and her laughter was shrill and cruel.

"There we are," she said. "The great Risto, half a man already."

"Pull me out!"

She leaned close, savoring it. "Do shut up, Risto. I forgot to mention a few details about traveling through time."

He twisted, trying to look past his vanishing body. Below his shoulders there was nothing, just white, as if he were being erased line by line. The pressure crushed in on him, and the sound grew louder, not wind but the force itself, insistent as a jet engine. Sweat rolled cold down his face.

Her eyes gleamed. "You're right, Risto. The crystal obeys your bloodline, not mine. That's why I needed you. Without it, you can't give the command. You can't say *show me home*. Without the tether, you'll drift forever, time will strip you apart, rebuild you into something else. And when it's finished, you won't remember who you are."

With a sharp tug she ripped the necklace over his head. She dangled it in front of him so he could see it swinging. "This is mine now."

The suction intensified. Rocks, dirt, and brittle pages from books tore free and spiraled into the disc. Orenda braced against the pull, hair and robes whipping around her. The necklace stretched outward in her grip, tugged by the same tide.

"Enjoy your new life," she taunted. "Maybe you'll wake up as someone better. Or maybe you won't wake at all."

Risto thrashed, fury pushing through his terror. "I'll find a way back, and when I do, I'll kill you."

"Without the stone? You won't even remember my name." She gripped his chin, forcing him to meet her eyes. "Goodbye, Risto."

And with that, she let go. The draw consumed him in an instant. He vanished into the disc like a bullet through glass.

The release hurled Orenda backward. She struck the floor hard, head snapping against the boards. Dazed, she sat up, hair wild, and watched the disc shrink, its edges unraveling into stars. She staggered to her feet, smiling through the pain. Adriel and Risto were gone, and the necklace was hers at last.

Her hands trembled as she raised the crystal. Fear

crept in despite the triumph, but she laughed it off. She turned.

The clay pot shattered against her skull, silencing her laughter, and she blacked out immediately. She lay beside the window, the necklace loose in her hand.

Daniel stood over her, dropping the shards from his hands. "That's the last laugh you'll have for a while."

He shoved her toward the shrinking disc, and as her head slipped into the glow, the pull caught hold, stuttering the collapse of the window. He tore the necklace from her palm and looped it over his own head. He pushed her deeper into the light.

The pull returned, steady and merciless. She slid in up to her knees, the glow swallowing her.

Daniel stared at the dwindling disc, three feet now, closing fast, Orenda almost gone. He backed up, chest heaving. "This one's for you, Risto."

Orenda disappeared.

Daniel sprinted and dove into the light just as it snapped shut, leaving the room in silence.

21

The headlights cut through the darkness, perfectly illuminating the road ahead as Tommy and Christopher drove toward the park. They kept a steady pace, and the engine was the only sound breaking the silence between them. Despite knowing that Hector and his crew would likely be at the park, Tommy and Christopher decided to go anyway. The park was neutral territory, no one group claimed ownership, and everyone was welcome there. It was like their own little slice of Switzerland, where conflicts were left at the entrance.

As they pulled up to the park, it was teeming with people. The place was massive, and it seemed like the entire student body had shown up. Bass came from three different directions, out of time with each other. Spilled beer sweetened the air, and somewhere a joint burned skunky and sharp.

"Well, I'm in the mood for a beer. How about you?" Tommy asked, already scanning the crowd.

"Hell yeah, but first, I need to take a leak," Christopher replied.

Both got out of the car, and Tommy headed straight for the crowd, while Christopher walked around to the rear of the car. He kept one eye on Tommy, who was already flirting with a group of girls, trying to charm his way into getting a drink. Christopher smiled, watching Tommy's antics. Typical Tommy: shoulders back, grin locked, selling confidence he barely owned.

When Christopher turned his attention back to his task, he was startled to see a man standing there, watching him. He jumped, nearly losing his balance while trying to finish up at the same time.

"Whoa, hey!" he said, fumbling with his zipper.

"Easy, kid. I didn't mean to spook you," the man said, taking a step back.

Christopher squared himself, still tense. "What's your deal, man? You think sneaking up on somebody like that's funny?"

The man shook his head, his voice steady. "No. I'm sorry. Name's Daniel. I just wanted a word with you." He hesitated, then added, "I knew your father."

Christopher narrowed his eyes. "My father?"

Daniel nodded.

He wiped his hand on his jeans, still cautious. "I'm Christopher," he said, keeping his distance.

"I know who you are," Daniel replied. His mouth twitched into the faintest smile. "I used to have a good friend named Christopher too." He motioned toward the park. "Walk with me a minute?"

Christopher hesitated but fell into step beside him, uneasy. "So, you knew my dad?"

"Yes," Daniel said quietly. "But there's more to it than that."

Up close, he looked road-tired, eyes rimmed in red, and hints of grey streaking his hair.

Christopher studied him, trying to place what it was in Daniel's voice that felt so strange, but trusting at the same time.

As they walked toward the crowd gathered around the keg, Tommy was already in full party mode, drawing attention to himself. "Whoooo hoooo!" he howled.

A girl nearby rolled her eyes. "Why's he howling like that?"

Christopher looked at Tommy, who lowered his head with a smile plastered on his face. "He's just practicing for the thrill of the chase," Christopher joked.

"Sounds like his mating call," Daniel added.

Tommy choked on his beer, sputtering with laughter

along with Christopher, while the girl shook her head and walked away. When Tommy finally regained his composure, Christopher handed a beer to Daniel.

"Thanks. It's been a while," Daniel said, raising his cup.

Christopher couldn't figure out what to make of him. He couldn't put his finger on why Daniel seemed so familiar, but it was hard to pin down. He felt that odd tug again, like hearing a song from childhood and not remembering the lyrics. As they tapped their cups together, Daniel studied him, weighing how much to say. He was surprised when Christopher spoke first.

"This might sound weird, but you seem really familiar. Have we met before? Maybe when I was a kid?"

Daniel hesitated, his mind racing. The noise of the park seemed to fade into the background as he searched for the right words.

"Actually, we have. I wasn't going to say anything. I thought you might think I was following you or something like that."

Christopher considered this for a moment, his brow furrowed. "Well... that's not the weirdest thing I've heard lately. I've been having these dreams, crazy stuff. They feel real sometimes, like I'm somewhere else. Sometimes I wake up and I swear I can still hear voices."

"What kind of voices?"

"I don't know. A woman, mostly. And sometimes… I don't know how to explain it. It's like someone's calling me, but I don't know who. Sounds stupid, right?"

Daniel shook his head. "No. Not stupid."

"You say that like you know something."

Daniel raised his cup again. "Just drink. Trust me, you're gonna need it." He drained the last of his beer.

Christopher finished his, then refilled their cups. He wasn't sure if Daniel was messing with him or not. Either way, it was unnerving.

"Ahhh, that hit the spot," Christopher said, letting out a long belch that seemed to come from his toes.

Daniel laughed.

They went to Daniel's truck, dropped the tailgate, and sat down. Daniel took a deep breath, ready to share the story he had been holding onto for so long. Metal groaned under their weight; the tailgate was cold through Christopher's jeans, grounding him.

"Wait a minute now," Christopher began. "You're saying that you're from the future, or another time I mean, this is confusing. And that we've known each other for a very long time, and that I'm from that same time or place?"

"Yes."

Christopher just stared at him in dismay.

Daniel maintained his seriousness, making Christopher

uncomfortable.

"I should probably go check on Tommy. He tends to get rowdy, if you know what I mean." He stood up and turned to walk away, but Daniel's words brought him back.

"Why do you keep the necklace hidden in your closet?"

Christopher tightened. He looked back at Daniel.

"How'd you know that? Are you a stalker?" He walked toward him now. "Have you been in my house?" He was beginning to get angry, though really he was just scared to death. "It's my mother, isn't it? You're after her. You're sick, man!"

He tossed his cup at Daniel, hitting him in the chest. Daniel made no attempt to defend himself. He stayed put.

"Stay away from my mother, and stay away from me!" he yelled, his index finger almost touching Daniel's nose. He turned to walk away, but he froze when Daniel spoke again.

"Your wife, Drisana, she misses you."

He stood with his back to Daniel, trying to catch his breath. The name meant nothing, but it rattled inside him like it belonged. Images flickered behind his eyes, a woman's laugh, and the touch of a hand. It was gone before he could grasp it, leaving only an ache.

"You know, the night you left, she was so happy to be

alive. You could see it in her face. I wish I were so lucky. By the way..." Daniel stepped closer. He leaned to Christopher's ear and whispered, "You're welcome. You know I knocked her out."

Christopher turned, his eyes glassy, his chest heaving.

Daniel didn't flinch. "Yeah, I knocked her out. That was after she let you go into the window. I took the necklace, threw her in, and made it through myself at the last second."

Christopher's mouth opened, but no words came. His knees trembled, his vision blurred. Tears welled for no reason he could explain. His mind filled with every question imaginable. *Just who is this man? Some sort of angel or prophet?*

Daniel placed his hands firmly on his shoulders, steadying him. "I came to save you, Risto."

The name struck like a hammer. The dam inside Christopher broke, and fragments rushed through him, yesterday and years past all colliding at once. His legs buckled under the weight of it, and darkness took him as he fell.

Daniel caught him and put him in the back of his truck, hoping this wouldn't last too long. He also wanted to keep him out of sight in case anyone walked by. He wiped Christopher's brow with the palm of his hand.

Ten minutes passed before he woke up. He slowly

rose up in the back of the truck, looking around. When he looked into Daniel's eyes, he finally recognized his old friend.

"Daniel," Risto said with a sigh of relief. He offered his hand to shake. They were glad to be together again. Relief hit like a deep cut being washed, sharp and stinging, but needed.

They stayed at the truck for the duration of the evening. They had a few more drinks, and Daniel caught Risto up to speed on everything. He started with the night Orenda had tricked him and lured him into the forest. How he had shown up at Orenda's house when she let him slip into the window, disappearing from their world. He explained how he knocked her out, and then crossed over.

He then explained how he had been with him since Risto was a child. He was the one who made it possible for him to find the necklace. He assured him that his wife, Drisana, and all the others in their village would be there waiting when they returned. Names and memories braided together, Risto remembered. He felt anger rising from what Orenda had done, and who she had become. Claudia. Everything made sense now.

"So when I return, how old will I be? Look at me now. I'm a kid," Risto said.

"No, when we return, you'll be the same age as when

you left, the night you were in Orenda's home."

"How is that possible?"

"Well, I'm not entirely sure. When we return, we'll just pick up where we left off. And maybe I won't be as grey either," he said smiling.

"And Drisana?"

"Don't worry, my friend. She'll be there, happy to see you."

"What do we do now? I'm ready to go home," Risto said.

"I couldn't agree with you more."

Just then they heard a scream from a girl. A fight had broken out, and they could see people starting to gather in a large group.

"It's Tommy," Daniel said.

"Tommy?" Risto said, remembering who he'd come to the party with.

They ran through the park, stumbling past beer cans and liquor bottles. They pushed their way through the crowd to the center. There, Hector and Tommy circled each other like tigers. Tommy had already been hit once, blood streaking down his cheek. The group of kids pushed in tighter, hungry for spectacle; someone yelled "Kick his ass!"

"What happened, Tommy?" Risto yelled.

"You stay out of this, chico! This is between me and

Señor Tommy," Hector said.

They lunged again, wrestling to the ground. Tommy finally got in a clean shot to Hector's nose. The crack echoed, and everyone heard it snap.

Daniel leaned toward Risto. "Listen to me. We've got to leave here, and fast."

"What about Tommy?"

"That's my point. We're taking him with us. I've got to save him."

"Take him where?" Risto paused briefly, trying to figure it out. "You're talking about the window, aren't you?"

Daniel just looked at him but didn't speak. They turned back as Tommy landed another hit on Hector. That one pissed Hector off. That's when he pulled the knife.

"That's it! You're gonna die," Hector snarled.

Tommy stood there with his face covered in blood, arms raised to block, worn out and barely standing.

The crowd started to chant, "Cut him, cut him, cut him!"

"These people are animals. I have to help!" Risto yelled.

"Trust me. This is it," Daniel said. He pulled the necklace from under his shirt. Risto couldn't believe what he was seeing.

"Where did you get that?"

Daniel didn't look at him. "The same place I told you before, the only place you ever thought it was safe. Now, stop wasting time." He grabbed Risto's hand and shoved the amulet from the necklace into his fist. "Say the words Risto, only you can do it."

Risto's eyes widened, his mouth falling open. He didn't know the words, yet somehow he did, they had been waiting inside him all along. He brought the crystal close to his lips and whispered to it. *"Show me home."*

Daniel looked just beyond the fight. Tommy and Hector were still circling. Hector's blade was suspended in front of his face, pointing toward Tommy. The air tightened, a pressure change before a storm.

"You're going down," Hector said, still moving.

As he started toward Tommy, Hector saw stars, sharp bursts that filled his vision. He shook his head, trying to clear it, but they only multiplied, spreading until the world swam. He knew Tommy hadn't hit him that hard.

Tommy began to notice the lights too, but figured it was from the blow he'd taken earlier. He was about to collapse, but then followed everyone else's eyes towards something behind him.

Hector stopped, stunned.

The air itself seemed to split. The brightest light rose out of nowhere, and the crowd fell back in fear. People pressed to both sides, staring as the window grew: three feet, four, five, six. Even Risto, who wanted to move, stood rooted to the ground, helpless as the circle expanded. He felt heat roll off it, dry and radiant. He watched as it grew, then his eyes caught something staring back at him just beyond the edge of the window—Claudia.

Tommy and Hector were frozen in place. Hector's knife dropped to his side. Tommy swayed like a bloody rag doll, half leaning, his eyes fixed on the impossible light. They stood with the rest of the student body in awe, enthralled by the size of the window, and the embers of light floating aimlessly.

Only Daniel knew what was really happening. He stood silent, watching the window grow to full strength. No one else even noticed him. He blended with the crowd, waiting for his moment.

When the window finally stopped, silence pressed down over the park. The window was at least twelve feet across, perfectly round, a solid wall of white. Daniel waited, patient as stone. The humming began, low at first, then rising. He knew it was time. If he waited any longer, the window would pull everyone into it.

Daniel looked at Risto, "The next few moments are crucial. You have to run with me, hold my hand and don't let go—no matter what."

Risto's eyes were searching Daniel for answers, but something inside him was coming forward, recalling. He nodded. "I won't let go."

Daniel broke from the crowd with Risto in tow, clinging to his hand for all he was worth. They ran hard toward the window, and Tommy.

Tommy, still barely standing, watched the floating embers of light hover randomly. He felt light-headed and faced forward again, shaking his head, to regain his composure. What he saw next was a full grown man coming into focus running straight at him, with Christopher right behind. He realized that the man intended to grab him, and braced for impact.

Daniel scooped Tommy up like he was nothing, bending him over underneath his right arm. He had a hold of him around the waist, looking like he had a human battering ram. Gasps chased them; someone dropped a cup that burst like a small grenade of foam.

Tommy was still in a daze and couldn't even seem to make himself fight free of Daniel's grasp. He raised his head as Daniel was running and couldn't see anything but white coming straight at him. His head shook with the rhythm of Daniel's pace. Blood dripped from his lip as they moved across the ground, and the hum of the window deepened as the light continued to glow bright.

When Daniel reached the edge of the window, he screamed, "Jump!"

Risto took a deep breath and jumped. Tommy

fearfully closed his eyes, unaware of what was about to happen.

All three of them disappeared into the light. The window stopped humming, then grew in size, just mere inches, taking a small breath, then blinked out of sight as if a switch had been turned off.

Everyone at the party had seen it. They drifted off in uneasy silence, none willing to put words to what they'd witnessed. By Monday, it would already be a rumor, blurred at the edges and stripped of names, passed in whispers. But as the crowd thinned, one person was missing—Claudia.

22

Risto landed on his feet but then dropped and rolled to a stop. He felt a little different, heavier. Disoriented, he replayed the last seconds, the white light, Daniel's shout, his own hand locking onto Daniel's. His bones felt older somehow, as though the years had pressed into him in a single breath.

He opened his eyes, and could see the tips of tall trees against the night sky. Everything was still; he heard nothing. The silence was unnerving, too quiet, the kind that seemed to swallow a man whole.

"Good, you didn't let go," Daniel said.

Risto sat up, stupefied, and looked at Daniel, who was crouched right in front of him. He was leaning over Tommy, who was lying on his back.

"Where are we?"

"The question is when are we?" Daniel said. "We are home my friend."

While Daniel spoke, Risto looked around. He was amazed at what had just happened. He tried to look beyond him at Tommy but couldn't see too clearly.

"Is Tommy okay?" Risto asked.

"Yes, he's going to be fine, I believe. I think he had just passed out before crossing over. He'll wake up soon."

Risto noticed something different about Tommy, though. He actually looked, or at least appeared, larger than normal. Also, his clothes weren't the same. He couldn't figure it out. The boyish awkwardness seemed stripped away, replaced with the frame of someone who'd carried weight, responsibility.

Daniel could tell Risto was noticing something different but hadn't quite figured it out yet.

"Mother of God," Risto said softly to himself. He was holding his hands out, giving them a good look. They were obviously more mature, seasoned. He then noticed his clothes. His pants were leather, not rock-n-roll leather, but the real stuff, fresh all-grain animal hide. His hair was longer, now touching his shoulders. He looked at Daniel, feeling queasy. The smell of hide clung to him; even his breath felt heavier, carrying dust from another life.

Daniel crawled to where Risto was and laid his hand on his shoulder. "You okay? Stay with me, Risto. Stay with me."

Risto seemed to regain his composure and laughed in disbelief, looking at Daniel. "We're really back. I can't believe it. Ha!"

"Yes, old friend, we're back."

"I've changed," Risto said, uneasy. "I'm not the boy anymore." Then, really looking at Daniel, "And you! You had grey earlier, but you're back as well—younger."

"We're the same age as when we left."

"It seems like a dream, like it never happened."

"Oh, it happened, all right. It will just take some getting used to. It's been a long time for both of us," Daniel explained.

"Yes, it has." Risto slowly stood to his feet.

He was taller, and he could feel it. His feelings were starting to come back to him slowly; things were beginning to feel more natural quickly.

He walked to the edge of the tree line and stopped, scanning the clearing as best he could. The moon was three-quarters full but provided enough light to see most everything. He couldn't believe how strong his sense of smell seemed to be. Maybe it was because the air wasn't polluted with the city life he had become accustomed to. The grass was sharp and sweet beneath his boots; the cold night tasted of pine and river water. He looked up to the sky in awe of the clarity of the stars, clear and sharp. He felt as though he could see past them if he held his eyes just right.

On the other side of the clearing, he caught faint hints of light, maybe people he knew, his village—Drisana. His heart fluttered when her name crossed his mind. He wanted to run straight to her, to see her face again, but the strangeness of those first moments held him back. He needed to steady himself, to let the reality of being home settle into him. He stopped and touched the tree next to him, tightening his grip; he felt the bark digging under his nails. He stared off through the trees, still feeling the anger inside towards Orenda. "I will find you," he said under his breath.

"You're going to be okay," he heard Daniel say.

Daniel was tending to Tommy, who was still passed out. Hector had socked it to him pretty good, but he would heal just as well. He smiled as he looked upon his old friend, who had been stuck in the body of a teenager for the past several years. Now, he finally looked himself again, and Daniel couldn't wait to tell Risto, if Risto could take it without passing out on him. He'd have to; they'd both have to. Many things had happened, but they were still the same people, people who had been asleep for a long time now. He was the one to wake them up, bring them back to reality.

He continued to wipe Tommy's brow. Then, finally,

he coughed and looked into Daniel's eyes.

Adriel was awake.

"You're going to be okay," Daniel said as he touched the side of Adriel's face.

Risto walked back to where Daniel and Tommy were.

"Is he going to be all right?" He stood looking over Daniel's shoulder but had no good vision of what was happening.

Daniel stood up and turned toward Risto, taking his shoulders in his hands. "Do you trust me?" He was so excited. His eyes were lit up with joy like Risto had never seen before. He couldn't quit smiling.

"Well, considering you've been my friend for years, in spite of the fact we've only known each other for about two hours now, yes, I trust you."

Adriel shifted uncomfortably. *Cough, cough.*

"Is he all right?" Risto asked.

"He's more than all right. I would like to introduce you to him." Daniel was staring into Risto's eyes but only saw complete confusion now.

"Why do you need to introduce us? I know Tommy very well," Risto said as he continually tried to look past Daniel to see what was happening.

"Yes, you do know Tommy..."

Cough, cough.

"...but you haven't seen this man in quite a while."

Daniel continued holding Risto by the shoulder but let go with the other, slowly turning to offer him the chance to step ahead.

"Risto, meet Adriel, your father."

Adriel had stood up by this point, and he and Risto were looking eye to eye.

Cough, cough.

Risto looked like he was trying to catch flies with his mouth, and Adriel maintained that serious fatherly look while trying not to cough.

Without another moment passing, Risto and Adriel embraced one another. They looked at each other closely, brought back from cheating death with another chance. The embrace was rough, but Risto clung to him as if time itself might tear them apart again.

As the night went on, the three stayed in the woods, too worn out to think of returning to Hope. They gathered near a fallen log, talking as the hours slipped by. They had decided to stay there to catch up on everything up to this point. It seemed to last for an eternity; the stories kept coming. Adriel spoke of the times when Risto was young and would greet him when he returned from hunting. They even talked about when Risto was older, when Adriel disappeared from his life, and what Orenda had done.

Risto told about the night Orenda had sent him back. All he could remember was being drawn into the window.

His last memory was seeing her face with that hideous grin and her hair all around it as he was being pulled in. He did mention that he wasn't positive, that it could have been a dream, but he thought he saw someone enter the room moments before slipping through.

Daniel confirmed again that it was no dream. He *had* come into the room at that moment and had seen Orenda holding on to him, then watched him slip away. He told how he was also responsible for Adriel and Risto meeting. He knew that they would be loyal friends and protect one another.

The necklace was the highlight of the evening. Each took turns passing it around. They looked upon it in amazement, staring deep into it, in awe of its power. The firelight caught its core, the blue heart pulsing like a living vein.

Risto stared into the fire, his brow creased. A thought gnawed at him, sharper the more he tried to ignore it. "Daniel... there's something I don't understand..."

Daniel looked up.

"I remember what Orenda told me that night. She said I wouldn't even know who I was without the necklace. If that's true, then how did we all cross over with our memories intact? Only you were wearing the necklace."

Daniel's face softened, almost amused. "That's why I grabbed your hand—skin to skin. I was already touching

Tommy, well, Adriel. The tether carried through us all. One link in the chain was enough."

Risto sat back, the explanation settling over him like a heavy cloak. "Skin to skin," he said to himself. "So I remember only because you held on."

"Because we held on to each other," Daniel said, nodding toward Adriel. "That's what made the difference."

Adriel, listening, reached out and put a hand on his son's arm. His voice was rough but steady. "Never let go again."

Daniel's pride showed in his eyes as he looked at them. "Well, men, here we are together again. We have survived and need to decide what to do next."

The men's faces were stern. They looked upon one another as the campfire continued to cast a glow on them. They knew it was time. Too much time had gone by, and Orenda needed to be stopped. Adriel was the first one to speak.

"I would rather not see Orenda anymore. I'll admit that she was a friend at one time, but she changed. For all I know, she never was a friend. She had planned this from the beginning."

Risto was a little surprised to hear his father speaking this way. He had always been a compassionate man and would never think of leaving someone behind, friend or foe.

"You don't feel we should find her, bring her back to Hope, then decide what needs to be done, justice?" Risto said.

"Justice?" Adriel questioned.

Daniel listened with Risto as Adriel spoke.

"That crazy woman sent me in that godforsaken window and then made my family believe I had been killed. Then she took you away from yours. The only justice she deserves is to be completely deserted and left behind. She has a new life now. I don't want to waste one more breath on the woman. For God's sake, she's a young woman like we were boys," he explained. "You didn't know who you were until Daniel told you."

Daniel looked toward the fire, knowing Adriel was right. He found a good poking stick so he could fumble with the coals.

Risto knew what his father meant and dared not to convince him otherwise. He had plenty of reasons to not want to go after Orenda either. He just felt that maybe together they would all want to bring her back and make her answer for what she did.

"And Daniel..." Adriel continued.

Daniel looked up.

"Bless this man for coming after both of us, for all he's done, for the time he's lost, too."

Risto nodded towards Daniel, thankful.

"What are we doing then, going home?" Daniel asked.

"I miss my wife terribly," Risto said. "Tell me exactly what you want or think we should do."

"Let's sleep here tonight and leave for home at first light," Adriel said.

Risto looked to Daniel for support. "Are you okay with this?"

Daniel nodded. "I think it's right. Maybe she's found a new life to suit her better. If that's the case, we've done her a favor. I say we go home."

Risto agreed. He trusted what they had to say, and in the end, he was even excited. He didn't feel bad anymore. He felt like Daniel had made a valid point that Orenda might be in a better place. "Ok, we'll leave at first light."

The fire was down to a few coals now, and without another word, they set up places to sleep. The silence was deep, broken only by the sigh of wind in the trees and the slow crackle of the last ember.

23

Claudia's body slammed hard against the ground. The impact drove the air from her lungs, and she lay there stunned, her chest heaving for breath. Pine needles dug into her palms as she clawed at the dirt. Slowly, she rolled onto her side. The scent of sap and earth filled her nostrils. Her ribs ached with each breath, and the throb in her skull made it feel as though the forest itself pulsed in time with her heartbeat.

She blinked, and shapes began to form. Trees towered above her, the night sky broken into slivers of starlight between their branches. Somewhere nearby, faint light flickered against the darkness. A fire.

She pushed herself upright, her body trembled. "Where am I?" she whispered, her voice hoarse. She staggered forward a few paces until she could see the fire more clearly through the trees. Three men sat gathered around the flames. She froze, crouching low, hidden in the shadows. Her eyes fixed on them. One of them she recognized, the man who had been with Christopher at the party. The others were strangers, yet something about them stirred her memory, sharp and painful. The tilt of a jaw, the cadence of a laugh, they pressed against her mind like names half-remembered in a dream. She crept closer, close enough to hear.

Their voices carried through the clearing. She listened, catching fragments at first, then more, until their entire conversation unfolded before her. Names struck like hammers: Risto. Adriel. Daniel. Her hand shot to her temple. Orenda. The name split her head. She gasped and staggered back against a tree.

"No..." she whispered, shaking her head. "No... yes. Yes, that's me." Her voice grew stronger. "I am Orenda."

Images surged, faces, a life she had lost. Hatred flared in her chest, sharp and pure. She bared her teeth toward the fire. Memories of power, of command, flickered in her blood like sparks.

"You left me. You thought you could cast me aside."

She squeezed her fists together, her nails tearing into her flesh.

"Where is my home? Where is Hope?" she hissed, turning in a slow circle, breathing the night air.

Recognition cut through her. "I'm here. I'm back."

The moonlight revealed her hands as she lifted them before her face. They were older now, hardened, hers again. She laughed softly. Wrinkles of cruelty creased the corners of her mouth.

"Claudia Montgomery... a shell. But me? I'm whole."

Their voices carried once more. She leaned closer, listening. When she heard their plan, not to come for her, to leave her behind forever, her body shook with rage.

"You cowards," she whispered. "You would abandon me?"

The fire burned lower. The men shifted, then grew silent, lying down for the night.

Orenda turned away and moved deeper into the forest. Each step steadied her, each breath pulled her further from Claudia's remnants. She stopped at the tree line and looked back. The men slept soundly, believing they had left her behind. A sinister smile spread across her face.

"You fools. I'm right here."

Her teeth caught the light like shards of bone. Her eyes glinted with a hunger that had waited years to be fed. Shadows bent oddly across her features, hiding what physical features had changed.

The face that watched was happy, happy to be back. And no one knew yet.

150

This face was evil. This face was Orenda.

Book 2

DECREE

1

It was a cool night, quiet beneath a cloudless sky where every star shone brightly. The solitary call of an owl echoed high within the forest canopy, its large eyes scanning the darkness. The owl fell silent, startled by a mysterious sound, not that of another creature, but something unidentifiable. Silence followed. Deep below the treetops, a dim light flickered through a window. This window belonged to a small, seemingly long-abandoned house. Inside, amidst a clutter of old books and cobwebs, a woman laughed.

Orenda kicked at the ground, laughing into her hands to muffle the sound, hopeful she remained unheard. Her arms flailed from side to side in childlike giddiness, barely containing her excitement.

"You're such a fool," she exclaimed through gritted

teeth. "You left me for dead in that dreadful place, in that awful body. You abandoned me to dwell among the maggots, with the forgotten men of Earth. But now I'm back. And best of all, no one knows I'm here. Except maybe you, Lucky." She addressed a coyote skull on a nearby shelf, her laughter resuming. The sockets of the skull seemed to drink in the candlelight, black holes staring back at her.

With a sudden swipe, she sent the skull crashing against the wall, where it disintegrated into dust. The smile vanished from her face, replaced by seething anger. She paced the room with her long-aged fingers brushing over old books, vials of potions, and trinkets, searching for the right idea to spring into her twisted mind.

"You've infested my life for too long, Risto, you and your friends. It's time to be done with you for good. You were lucky to have your friends keeping such a close eye on you. They were the ones who saved you. You certainly didn't save yourself."

Her fingers paused atop a book. She looked down, wiped the dust from the cover, and pushed it aside to reveal another hidden beneath.

"There you are," she murmured, picking it up carefully and caressing it like a long-lost pet. "I haven't seen you for a long time, my friend. Together we will create miracles. Together we will bring peace to all."

She hugged the book tightly against her chest, then found a spot on the floor near the pit where she and Risto had dove into that other time. She crossed her legs, placed the book in her lap, laid her hands on the cover, and closed her eyes. She whispered a dark call for help, almost inaudible, summoning something not of this world. The air thickened around her as candle flames bowed inward, as though drawn to the pit.

When she finished, she opened the book and let her fingers glide across the pages, eyes still shut. A smile began to form. When she opened her eyes, her gaze filled with fiery intensity and the smile twisted into a snarl. Her laughter returned, louder and more potent than before. It rattled the shelves, and shook dust from the rafters.

"Yes. Yes. Of course," she howled into the night. "It's so much clearer now. Damn all of you!"

Somewhere deep in the forest, an owl spread its wings and flew away. The beating of its wings was frantic, as though even the creature of night wanted no part of what had awakened.

Evil was stirring.

2

The sun was touching Risto's face when he awoke. He could not recall a day quite as magnificent, and if he had, it seemed a distant memory. His prolonged absence, both mental and physical, from this place had dulled his memories.

Standing by the window, he observed the early risers embarking on their daily routines. As his eyes adjusted, a sense of contentment washed over him. He had returned home with his friends and family intact, and, most importantly, to rediscover himself.

For Risto and his companions, it felt as though years had passed, while for the rest of the world, nothing had changed at all. Being displaced in another time and having spent seven years growing up with another family weighed heavily on his mind. Now back where he belonged with

Adriel, Risto could not help but think of the families they had left behind, the ones who had raised Christopher and Tommy. The pain he might have caused those people, particularly Christopher's mother, whom he dearly loved, troubled him deeply. Knowing the anguish of potentially losing a child, he could only imagine the agony she must be enduring.

Despite feeling at home, something was wrong deep within him, which he could not pinpoint.

"Hey."

Turning, Risto was greeted by a sight more beautiful than any sunrise—Drisana. He smiled warmly at her.

"How long have you been up?" she inquired.

"Only a little while. Did you sleep well?"

"Of course." Drisana stretched. "I had you beside me. You're all I need for a good night's sleep."

He looked back outside, then closed his eyes, basking in the sunlight. Her voice drew him back.

"Are you alright?"

Risto inhaled deeply. "I'm fine. I feel good, but I need to talk to you about something important. It's going to be difficult."

"I know. It's amazing, isn't it? Your father. He's alive!" Drisana exclaimed, placing her hands on his shoulders.

Risto nodded and smiled. "It is amazing. You haven't told anyone yet, right? Just like we discussed?"

"No, I haven't said a word. He's still with Daniel. Is something wrong?"

Risto said nothing for a moment, then asked, "What do you remember most about last night? You spoke with Orenda and me in the forest. Did anything seem odd to you, or stand out?"

"I'm not sure what you mean. Orenda is odd, so should my answer be yes? You're testing me, right?" she replied, puzzled.

Realizing the complexity of the situation, Risto knew he had to make her understand the gravity of what had transpired. He needed to reveal who Orenda truly was and her capabilities, and also what he had discovered about himself and his control over the necklace.

"With all the celebrating, there never seemed to be a good time to tell you about what happened," Risto explained. He rubbed his chin, feeling the stubble, as he studied her eyes.

She crossed the room and sat on the edge of the bed, signaling for him to join her.

Risto knew she was his soulmate and could handle anything he needed to share. He sat beside her, taking her hand.

"It's time you know the truth," he began, his voice steady.

Drisana's face tensed in anticipation.

"Not just about last night," he said. "About everything."

Her eyes searched his face. "What do you mean?"

He swallowed hard, his voice low and strained.

"Drisana... *she* caused all of this. Orenda. Everything I'm about to tell you started with her. She made me believe she was you. She tricked me, drew me in, and when I was helpless, she sent me back in time, or another place in time. I don't know how to say. None of what happened was by my choice."

He steadied himself.

"Drisana. For you, it was only a night. But for me..." his voice wavered before he found strength again. "For me, seven years passed. Seven long years in another life. I was taken, displaced in time. I lived with another family. I grew older while, to you, everything stayed the same. You went on as though I had never left."

Her lips parted, but no sound came. She clutched his hand tighter, as though grounding herself in his presence.

"There was a woman who raised me as her own," he continued softly. "Her name was Jen... my mother. I grew up with her, believing I was her son, Christopher. And there was another boy, Tommy. He lived with his own parents, but we were inseparable, like brothers. They became my family. I loved them. And when I returned here, it was as though none of it existed. But it did. I can

159

still see their faces. I can still feel the pain of leaving them behind."

His voice cracked, grief weighing on each word.

"Risto..." Drisana whispered, her eyes glistening. "That's why you look so burdened."

He nodded. "I couldn't carry it alone anymore. I need you to know me—all of me. What I've done, what I've seen, will stay with me forever. The truth, even if it makes no sense, even if it goes against your memories, is still the truth.

She brushed her thumb gently across his knuckles, silent but listening. "You said something about her, making you believe she was me. What did that mean?"

Risto drew a breath.

He explained how Orenda had deceived him in the forest. He described how she manipulated time, restoring everything to normal without Drisana realizing anything was amiss.

She listened intently, her expression a mixture of fright and concern.

"Just knowing you might have been with her is killing me," she admitted. "But if what you're saying is true, you couldn't have known until it was too late, right?"

"Correct," he assured. "I didn't know it was her until she revealed herself, right after you left."

"I just don't know, Risto. This was just last night to

me. The only thing I remember was talking to both of you. You were acting strange, quiet in fact. Then I returned to the party because Orenda asked me to," she confessed.

He listened.

She repeated the situation, really just to understand. "You're saying I saw you with Orenda, that I caught you. Why would you tell me this? Why make it up?"

"Drisana, I'm not making it up. Why would I go through the trouble of telling you if it weren't true?"

"I don't know. Something doesn't seem right," she said, her gaze piercing.

"You're right. It isn't right. It's unnatural. But it did happen. You don't think I actually did something with Orenda, do you?" he asked, a note of desperation in his voice.

She remained silent, offering only a look. Risto moved closer, earnestly trying to reason with her.

"Think about it. If all you remember is saying hello and leaving, and I wanted to get away with it, why would I tell you anything at all? Why not keep quiet?"

Drisana knew he was right but said nothing immediately. She stood up and paced the room, deep in thought.

"I need some time alone, to think. I'm not mad, just very confused."

"That's understandable."

She kissed him on the forehead and left the room, leaving Risto alone with his thoughts, wondering if revealing the truth had been worth the upheaval.

He sat quietly, the weight of guilt and unresolved years tugging at him. Despite the turmoil, he felt it was essential that Drisana knew everything, not just for their sake, but to understand the threat Orenda had posed to them all.

Gathering himself, Risto decided to seek out his father, Adriel, hoping he could provide clarity for the storm still raging inside him.

3

When Risto stepped outside, it was as if his recent conversation with Drisana had vanished, and being home was all that mattered. Deep down, he knew this was right; this was where he belonged. As he watched several townspeople going about their daily routines, Risto felt a reluctance to socialize. He needed to reach Adriel as soon as possible and preferred to do so unnoticed.

Making a sharp left, he veered behind his house and cut through the dense woodland that bordered it. This route, weaving through the forest like a crescent moon, offered a quicker, unseen path to Daniel's house.

Upon arrival, he found Adriel and Daniel enjoying each other's company in the main room. Risto's sudden appearance startled them, with Daniel leaping up in alarm, ready for an unexpected threat.

"There you go again, trying to be the smart one, sneaking around. Why not use the front?" Daniel scolded.

"I'm trying to avoid complications," Risto explained, gesturing toward the front where several townspeople passed by, all curious about Adriel's miraculous return.

Daniel resettled himself. "You've been gone a long time, Adriel. What will we tell them?"

"The truth," Risto replied, his eyes tracking the bystanders outside.

"Do you think that's wise, son?" Adriel asked, skeptical of the implications given his unchanged appearance. "I mean, I look exactly the same as I did the day I left. To them, I've been dead nearly twenty years. How could we possibly explain that?"

Daniel leaned forward, steady in his tone. "That's true, to Hope, you were gone two decades. But the tether changes everything. You didn't return to the moment you left. When Risto and I pulled you through, you came with us, into *this* time, into *our* present. Without the tether, yes, you would've snapped back to the night you vanished. But now..."

"It makes the most sense," Risto affirmed. "Besides, the people of Hope need to understand what Orenda did. They deserve to know the whole truth about her."

"You're right," Adriel agreed, giving it thought. "They should know the truth."

Daniel nodded.

"It's settled then. We'll make an announcement this afternoon. I'll explain everything," Risto declared, though his tone carried a trace of apprehension.

Trying to lighten the mood, Daniel offered, "How about a cup of ale? That's sure to ease your mind before you address the town."

Risto accepted, his mind clearly preoccupied with other thoughts.

Adriel wasted no time asking. "What's on your mind, son? This should be a happy time for you, back in Hope, away from Orenda. I've been gone so long now, people look to you for answers. They need someone to lead them, someone they trust."

Risto scoffed and rubbed the back of his neck.

"Don't kid yourself," Adriel continued. "You've grown in many ways. I can see it in you. You're a good man, and they know it too."

Risto revealed his inner conflict. "If I'm such a strong leader, why am I plagued by this pain, this—resentment?"

"You shouldn't have any resentment for being home, where you belong. You..."

"I don't resent being here. I resent leaving my old life, leaving my mother behind," Risto interrupted.

Adriel's face tightened. "What? Jen was a fine woman, and raised you well. She did all she could on her own, but she was strong, and I commend her for that. But son, you have to move on."

"How can I just move on like nothing happened? She was a part of my life, and I hers. What about you and your parents? Don't you feel bad for not being there? They loved you and raised you. Do you ever think about what it cost them, losing you like that?"

"They're not my true parents," Adriel said.

"I understand that, but they did raise you until the time you left. I think that covers the issue that they are, or were your parents."

"No, they're not!" Adriel shouted, reflecting no emotional attachment to his foster parents.

The room fell into a tense silence, broken only when Daniel slinked into the room with three cups of ale. He set them on the table that divided Risto and his father. "Ale?" he said, looking up between them, as if testing whether it was safe to breathe.

Nobody moved. Daniel looked back and forth from Adriel to Risto, then down at the cups, uncertain whether he should remove himself from the situation or just start drinking.

After a brief, awkward pause, and while maintaining eye contact with his father, Risto downed his drink in a few gulps and wiped his mouth.

"I have some things I need to take care of, so I'll leave

you to it."

"Oh? Where will you go?" Daniel asked, smiling.

"I have some unfinished business to attend to," he said, still looking at Adriel.

"But what about the gathering this afternoon? You were going to speak. Will you be back in time?" Daniel said, concerned.

"I'll do my best, but if I'm not…" Risto trailed off, leaving the responsibility implicitly to his father.

Without another word, he walked out the front door and into a crowd of inquisitive townspeople. Despite their barrage of questions, Risto pressed forward, his mind set on his undisclosed tasks.

Inside, Daniel and Adriel watched him leave, uncertainty hanging in the air. The two stood by the window, silent, following Risto's figure as he walked through the crowd. Daniel tried to salvage some normalcy in the tense moment and made his offer again, eyes still on the glass.

"Ale?"

4

Orenda closed the ancient book resting on a podium sculpted to resemble a raven. Its wings were spread wide in support of the heavy volume, and its sharp-clawed feet were planted firmly on the ground. Its beak was thrust forward as if to seize any listener brave enough to come closer.

Exhausted and drenched in sweat, she leaned on the podium, clutching the book's edges for support. A laugh of disbelief and exhilaration escaped her lips. She had ventured into realms of magic she had only dreamed of, pushing her limits, fully aware of the dangers and irreversible consequences that might follow. Yet, if her plans succeeded, she would ascend to a new pinnacle of forbidden knowledge.

Having spent the entire night immersed in complex

rituals, Orenda meticulously pronounced each mystic syllable and executed every gesture with precision, aware that any misstep could lead to catastrophic self-destruction. As dawn's first light crept through the windows, she extinguished the dwindling candles, their wax spilling out in intricate patterns. Overcome by fatigue, she crawled into her bed and fell asleep within seconds, haunted by the uncertainty of her actions' effectiveness.

As midday approached, a soft breeze played among the treetops. Suddenly, a horrific scream shattered the tranquility. Orenda jolted awake, clutching the bed sheets, her body wracked with unbearable pain. She howled at the ceiling, rolling back and forth in a futile attempt to escape the agony.

"What are you? What is this pain? What is this magic?" she cried out, pleading for forgiveness from unseen forces she feared she had inadvertently summoned.

The pain was relentless, manifesting as deep abdominal cramps that made her double over. It migrated unpredictably, creating the sensation of something crawling beneath her skin, causing it to ripple and bulge. In desperation, Orenda collapsed near the edge of the pit, her body convulsing violently. She could hear her own bones cracking under the strain, prompting another scream of anguish.

"No! Why?" she howled.

The pain was so intense she nearly vomited while trying to stabilize herself on her hands and knees. The sound that escaped her mouth was bark-like, more of a grunt, and her eyes rolled back into her skull. The bones in her back and along her spine began to move.

As she struggled, the skin on her back darkened, turning an eerie black. The transformation was grotesque; the surface of her skin began to morph, forming the distinct silhouette of a creature known in legend as the Narloc, a being rumored to traverse the realms between worlds, loyal only to those who could summon and control them.

The creature's form became increasingly defined against her back. Two small, clawed feet emerged near her tailbone, followed by long, slender legs that aligned with her spine. Eyes, vivid green and luminescent, appeared amidst the shifting patterns. Her back swelled as the creature inside her fought to break free. With a final, excruciating tear, the Narloc detached itself from Orenda.

The creature was a ghastly sight, its body elongated with bat-like wings veined and taut, capable of crawling on the ground with its small, powerful claws. It moved close to the floor, almost rubbing its stomach as it crawled. The Narloc pulled itself forward with its claws, while its back feet pushed in quick, stuttering bursts. Though its movements appeared unstable, they were anything but, every step precise.

It hissed as it surveyed its surroundings, its presence an ominous testament to Orenda's dark dealings.

No sooner had the first Narloc freed itself than another began its painful emergence from Orenda's convulsing form. The first creature lingered near the pit, watching as its kin joined it in the dimly lit room.

Orenda lay motionless, her body a mere husk from which these dark entities had been born, faint smoke rising from the burns left by their fiery exit.

The Narlocs, now free, positioned themselves with deliberate, unsettling movements. Their very presence was a chilling fulfillment of Orenda's most dangerous creation.

5

Risto navigated through the crowd, largely unnoticed despite who he was. One person reached out and touched his shoulder, trying to speak with him, but he gently pushed the hand away.

"Please, not now. I have business to tend to."

He continued on his way, the crowd parting, respecting his need for space and knowing their questions would eventually be answered.

He wandered away from Hope, seeking solitude. A deep inner conflict made him reject the comforting notions of being back home. As Risto continued to walk, his only desire was to escape from Hope, from everyone. He needed time to process everything that had happened, but all he could find in his reflections were pain and sorrow for his mother Jen, and for Tommy's parents. He fantasized about returning to that other time to visit Jen, but he swiftly pushed those thoughts aside.

Thoughts of his father weighed heavily on him, compounding his confusion and anguish. His sorrow soon turned into a smoldering anger, and he felt a desperate need to act.

"I know how I should feel," he muttered, haunted by the noise of their voices and the incessant advice on how he should manage his feelings.

Risto veered south, and soon, he discovered a small clearing in the forest, marked by a large boulder in a treeless patch. He leaned against the boulder, stretching his legs, and felt a wave of relief. The stone was still warm from the day's sun, pressing heat through him. The quiet was fragile, broken only by the drone of insects and the occasional creak of shifting branches. The only other sounds were those faintly drifting from Hope, where the townspeople were likely preparing for the evening's festivities. The town enjoyed any excuse for a celebration, and tonight would be no exception.

Beyond the boulder, the ground sloped down toward a small creek, a shadow of its former self. He scoffed, remembering days when the creek was more full and bustling with the laughter of playing children. Now its trickle sounded thin, almost embarrassed, winding weakly around pebbles.

He followed the creek south until he reached a familiar childhood place, a fort-like spot under a large oak tree where the creek had eroded the earth away, exposing its roots. The spot had always offered cool shade and a respite from the summer heat. Settling there, Risto leaned back, trying to calm his racing thoughts.

He was thankful to be back with Drisana, yet the thought of Jen's loneliness still lingered. Each time he considered stepping through the window to see her, he froze. How could he explain being her son, now a grown man? The risk of not being recognized, or the potential danger if she reacted defensively worried him.

Reaching into his vest, he pulled out the necklace with the powerful amulet, hidden in a sewn pocket. He had not worn it since the night Orenda had stolen it. Having retrieved it from Daniel, he now kept it close but out of sight. Risto decided he was ready. He *was* going to do it— see Jen. He wanted to at least glimpse her current situation.

Holding the crystal, he whispered, "Show me Jen." A portal-like window appeared above the creek. Initially black, it gradually brightened to silver. Sunlight reflected off it, momentarily blinding him. When his vision cleared, he saw a large window with a mirror-like surface. He stood before it, the silence broken only by the familiar hum, starting faint.

He checked his surroundings for any followers as the pull from the window intensified. Tiny streams of water moved toward it, vaporizing before they could reach it.

"I have to do this. I *want* to do this. You deserve to know what happened to me, to all of us," he resolved, staring into the window.

As he prepared to step through, he realized he still wore his sword. Knowing it could cause trouble, he slid it deep into the hollow beneath the oak's exposed roots, hidden in the shadowed space like a tree-cave. The blade scraped softly against the wood and dirt, a secret left behind in the dark soil, as if the earth itself were keeping watch. Then he stepped through the window. It closed instantly, restoring quiet to the forest. The wind died down, the trees stilled, and the creek resumed its quiet flow. The forest floor's shadows became still, all except one shadow on a rock, draped across the tree roots where Risto had sat.

As tranquility returned, that shadow, the single Narloc, slowly raised its head, its wings unfurling as it surveyed its new surroundings.

6

Risto raised his head, finding himself on one knee. He could not recall the details of the jump, it had been instantaneous. As he was momentarily blinded by the sunlight, he let his eyes adjust and began recognizing familiar places.

He was about a quarter mile from the high school he and Tommy had attended, which meant the neighborhood where they had lived was just south of there. Making a beeline toward his old neighborhood, Risto's heart flooded with memories long thought forgotten. Flashbacks of him and Tommy riding their bikes to the local store for fountain drinks and candy brought a smile to his face. The memory even carried a phantom taste, cheap cherry syrup at the bottom of a wax cup, and sugar lingering on his tongue as Tommy raced him back down the cracked sidewalk.

Then he thought of his mother, Jen. Understanding what had really been going on all those years struck him anew, filling him with immense love for her. He also realized the daunting challenge of explaining to her who he really was. Would she call the cops? Would she believe him? If things got out of hand, he still had the necklace to fall back on, even if using it would raise questions for years to come.

He arrived at the parking lot next to the high school and cut across it toward the main road that divided his old neighborhood from the school. The lot bore the usual marks of time, graffiti from seniors in fading colors, broken glass, bottle caps, and a lost pen. On the high school wall, a homecoming mural still clung, its colors sun-bleached. He and Tommy were supposed to be there. That time was gone.

Reaching the intersection, Risto pushed the crossing button. As cars whizzed by, throwing hot air in his direction, he briefly considered jaywalking but decided against it, wary of attracting police attention. Finally, the light turned red, and the pedestrian signal flashed green. Just as he was about to step into the street, two young boys playing tag darted past him. He froze in place as their sneakers slapped the pavement, and their laughter trailed behind them.

He quickly crossed, avoiding eye contact with the drivers who seemed to be sizing him up. Once safely on the other side, he felt a sense of relief as the traffic resumed. Now, his thoughts turned solely to Jen. He was only two houses away from his childhood home, overwhelmed with emotions and memories.

There she was, alone in the front yard, tending to her flowerbed. The smell of turned soil drifted across the yard, carrying on a faint breeze. His throat tightened, and a tear escaped as he watched her work. This was his mother, not by birth but through the years of care she had given him. She had chosen to raise him, sacrificing much. Adriel's dismissal of her significance had angered him, and he knew better than to try to explain things to Mr. and Mrs. Price about Tommy. His only concern now was Jen.

As he approached, she paused in her gardening, sensing something. She hesitated, then resumed, only to stop again and turn slowly. Dropping her shovel in uncertainty, she locked eyes with Risto.

"Can I help you?" she asked, her voice steady but curious.

Carefully walking through the grass, Risto maintained a respectful distance to keep her at ease. He nodded. "Hello, Jen."

She frowned, tilting her head. "Do I know you? You seem... familiar somehow."

Risto's heart pounded. This was the moment.

"Think back," he said softly. "Your son. The boy who lived here with you. Christopher.

She took a sharp breath, but her eyes remained uncertain.

He stepped closer, his voice trembling now. "You taught me to ride my bike in that driveway. You used to pack peanut butter sandwiches with the crust cut off because I wouldn't eat it otherwise. You told me to have faith, even in the darkest times."

Her face shifted with shock and confusion, then dawning recognition. She staggered back, and her hands trembled. "Christopher...? No... that can't be..."

"It's me, Mom," Risto whispered. "I know it makes no sense, but it's me. I've wanted this moment for so long, but I was afraid you wouldn't believe me. Afraid you'd think I was crazy, or some stranger making it up. But I remember, and so do you, don't you?"

Jen pressed a hand to her mouth, tears forming in her eyes. "My God. I do remember. I don't know how, but I do."

Risto smiled through his own tears and stepped closer, placing a hand on her shoulder. She responded by pulling him into a tight hug, which he returned with relief. After a moment, he touched the side of her face gently. "There is much to talk about."

"Come inside. Let me make you something, then we'll talk," she offered, her voice still trembling as she led him into the house.

Inside, Risto and Jen spoke for hours. He recounted everything, from finding the necklace in high school to his recent return. She listened intently, offering him lunch and a beer, which he accepted despite usually preferring stronger brews like Daniel's homemade ale. The clink of the bottle on the table, the smell of the house, these small things he felt he took for granted came rushing back to him, overloading his senses. There was so much to tell, and by the time he finished his story, he felt emotionally drained.

"What's wrong?" she asked. "You've given me all this information, but you seem sad."

"I feel lost. After all I've been through and seen, and now finally getting back to you and explaining, I thought that would ease some of my worries. But I still feel lost. What's the point of all of this?"

"Remember what I taught you? Faith?" she replied, not pushing him toward any specific belief but encouraging him to find comfort in something greater.

"Oh Lord!"

"Now you've got it," Jen laughed, playing along.

"That's not what I meant," he said, appreciating her effort to lighten the mood. "I'm not sure about faith, but I am sure about the sword at my side and my gut. I trust them both, a lot."

"I believe you. I can see it in your eyes. But just remember, someday you may not have your sword. Someday, faith may be all you have. Faith is strong enough to bring down any sword from any man," Jen advised, hopeful that he would find his own path to peace.

As they continued talking, she eventually asked, "How long are you staying?"

"I've been here too long as it is, and I should probably return," Risto admitted, feeling that the longer he stayed, the harder it would be to leave.

She nodded, accepting his decision with a mixture of sadness and understanding. "You're a handsome man, and I'm glad you've found someone that makes you happy. So, any children in your future? Do I have the chance of becoming a grandmother?"

"Let's not get too excited now. It might be a little soon for that."

"Family is never too soon, Risto. Remember what I taught you—faith. It's there. You just need to listen to it. Things will work out," she reassured him.

He hugged his mother tightly, not wanting to let go. She cried softly, her love for him clear.

"I love you, Mom."

"I love you too." She wiped her eyes. "Now get out of

here and go live the life you're supposed to. Make me proud, and only return if you truly can. I'll be fine knowing you're good."

With a final kiss, Risto wiped a single tear from her cheek. The moment seared into him, the faint powder of soil still on her fingers, and the smell of her shampoo burned into him. He left, carrying with him the love and strength from his mother, ready to face whatever the future held.

Risto collapsed onto the ground, exhausted. Crawling into the hollow beneath the tree, he let his eyes adjust before pushing on. He needed to process everything that had happened and reflect on his conversation with Jen.

A breeze caressed his face, the air cool against his skin. Above, the trees swayed gracefully, their branches framing patches of sky where the sun hid behind thick clouds. It looked like rain might fall soon. As Risto watched the sky, an uneasy feeling stirred within him. Something felt off, as if something had changed.

He sprang up and inspected his surroundings carefully, making sure he had not been transported elsewhere. Everything appeared normal, the creek, the trees, but it all felt different somehow, as if a shadow lingered just beyond his sight.

Drisana flashed through his thoughts, bringing with her a sense of impending doom. Quickly, he hid the necklace back in his vest and unearthed his sword from the dirt, strapping it around his waist before running back to Hope with a sense of urgency.

As he approached the town, he slowed his pace, his heavy breathing drawing concerned glances from a few townspeople.

"You okay, Risto?" one voice called out.

"Yes, I'm fine. Have you seen my wife?"

"Not recently, but I'm sure she's around," another answered.

Risto nodded his thanks and continued, only to be stopped by his father's voice.

"Risto," Adriel called, approaching from the opposite direction. "What's wrong, son? You look like you've seen a ghost."

"Maybe I have," he muttered, eyes darting past his father.

"Don't be that way, son. Talk to me," Adriel said calmly.

"Where's Drisana? I feel as if something's wrong."

"She's fine. I just saw her heading toward the stream with her friends. They were all in good spirits."

Despite his father's words, Risto's expression remained fraught with concern as he scanned the area, desperate to find Drisana.

"I assure you that Drisana's okay. Trust me," Adriel reiterated.

Risto nodded, but his unease persisted. "Something's happened. I'm not sure what, but something's different."

Adriel studied his son closely. "Risto, you seem like a lost child, terrified about something. What happened?"

Risto's eyes found his father, but looked away quickly.

"You went and saw her, didn't you? Jen?" Adriel guessed, his expression tightening.

"Yes."

Adriel's brow fell loose. He closed his eyes, a moment of sadness filled with worry. "You may have changed our future, Risto, our present, our now. It could be different in some way. This may be why you feel different, or scared."

Now Adriel was scanning their surroundings. "I can't believe you did this. All because you felt bad and wanted her to know the truth. I hope it was worth it."

"It was worth it, and I'd do it again."

"Well, good for you. I hope for all of us that we're safe and our future is stable. You had better hope that too," Adriel said before walking away.

Risto grabbed his arm, his eyes conveying deep sadness. "Father, when I got back, through the window, I mean, I felt as if Hope were in danger. I truly believe that what I did had nothing to do with that feeling. It's something else."

Adriel listened intently, pushing past his disappointment. "What do you mean, something else?"

"Orenda," Risto said gravely.

Adriel swallowed hard.

"I believe that Orenda is, or has already, done something. I don't know how it could even be possible, but that's what I feel in my gut. She's still among us somehow."

"She's here? You've seen her?"

"No, I didn't say that. But I can feel her, and I can't explain why."

"Okay, hold on. Talk to me first about seeing your mother, Jen. What happened there? Maybe that will help me understand."

"Honestly, there isn't much to tell. I found her at home and we spoke for about an hour. She invited me in. Everything was smooth, without incident," Risto recounted.

"How did she react to what you told her about yourself? About us?" Adriel asked.

"She was relieved to find out that I, well, that we, were okay. She took it very well and said something along the lines of knowing I was different and meant for something great," he shared.

Adriel nodded. "Go on."

"That was really it. She wasn't shocked at all, and more or less told me I was welcome anytime if I wanted to return, but understood if I couldn't."

Adriel thought for a moment. "Please don't take this wrong, but do you think it was really her? Do you think it's possible somehow that Orenda knew you were returning and tricked you?"

Risto considered this.

"You know she did it before, and you never knew," Adriel added.

"No, I don't believe that. I believe I would have known."

"Okay," Adriel accepted, though he remained concerned. "We better get indoors. Several people are starting to take notice, and I'm not ready to talk to everyone until later this evening."

Risto agreed, then they walked together toward Daniel's house.

"Son, I admire what you did. The courage, I mean. Going back to talk to your mother was a brave thing, and I understand why you did it. You're a better man for that."

Risto smiled, touched by his father's words. "Does that mean you've changed your mind and you're considering doing the same for Mr. and Mrs. Price?"

Adriel scratched at the back of his neck, hesitating. "Listen, I believe this is where we need to accept the fact that we agree to disagree. I don't feel it necessary to go back, but I don't want to fight with you about it either."

"I understand. I won't be mad," Risto assured him.

"It was a brave thing that you did. You look so sad though. Ever since we returned, you just haven't seemed the same. Is there anything I can do to help? I just want to know that you're okay."

"I do feel really lost," Risto confessed. "Ever since we came home, I've felt a pit in my stomach, like there's more."

"More?"

"I'm not sure how to explain it. It's like I just don't believe in anything," he admitted.

"What about God?"

Risto scoffed. "God? Right now I don't have time to think about God, and I'm sure he has more going on than me and my whining."

Adriel stopped and took his son by the shoulders, looking him in the eyes.

"Don't say that. You've lost your faith, son. You need to find it, or you *will* be lost. Don't be so hard on yourself. We've all been through a lot, but it's time we take back our lives and move forward."

Risto looked down, avoiding his father's gaze to prevent tears.

"Son, this is partly why I didn't want to return to

speak to Mr. and Mrs. Price. I've accepted this moment and don't want to dwell on the past anymore. Let's concentrate on the *now*. I feel like you take too much on yourself. You can't save everyone, and you certainly can't make people feel what you want them to feel. These things are beyond your control."

He lifted Risto's chin to meet his gaze. "Please take care of your wife. Start fresh and move forward. That's what's important. Everything else will work out."

"I'll do my best. And thank you."

Adriel hugged his son. "Stay with me. I need to go over a few things at Daniel's before the gathering. Be with us, and rest your thoughts."

"That sounds good, but I'll catch up. There's just one more thing I need to do," he replied. Seeing the concern in his father's eyes, he added, "It's okay. I'll be there soon."

Adriel patted his son on the back. "Good. Be careful."

Risto watched his father leave, then turned and headed back out of town, determined to resolve his unease.

8

Orenda stood in the corner, watching the Narlocs multiply. From the initial two, each spawned two more, continuing their sinister replication throughout the day. They writhed like wet shadows peeling away from one another, each birth accompanied by a hiss that rattled the walls. Though she could halt their growth at any moment, greed had taken over, her desire for more overwhelmed her. Wrapped in a wet blanket that soothed the burns from the Narlocs' emergence, she watched with a childlike grin, delighted by her burgeoning army.

The Narlocs, perfectly camouflaged, merged into shadows, twisting and shaping, able to confuse their prey. Their bodies shimmered faintly when they moved, like heat rising from stone, so that even when hidden, they bent the air around them. The room filled with the hiss of the creatures and the cries of the newly formed, echoing a sinister chorus.

Risto marched swiftly away from town, his sword rhythmically tapping against his leg. The encounter with Orenda in the park, where she had lived as Claudia, unsettled him. It seemed impossible that she could have followed him through the window, yet the possibility nagged at him. Every step he took in the forest felt heavier, as though the trees themselves pressed closer, listening. Lost in thought, he navigated the familiar forest paths to Orenda's house, a place he had known since childhood.

As the warmth of the afternoon settled, Risto approached the house, noting movement through a small window. His heart sank. "No, it can't be," he said. Yet, despite what he wanted to believe, he knew he was in the right place. The realization filled him with dread.

"How did you manage it, and what have you done this time?" he whispered, bracing for the worst as he approached the door.

Inside, Orenda surveyed the throng of Narlocs filling her small home. Their numbers had reached hundreds, perhaps even thousands, each capable of shifting size and merging into darkness. She beamed, sensing Risto's presence even before the scrape of his sword reached her ears.

"Hide, my friends, I will let you have your fun soon enough."

The Narlocs vanished in seconds, leaving the room eerily quiet, the kind of silence that prickled the skin.

Risto burst through the door, sword in hand, the smell of smoke and a strange odor hitting him immediately. It was the reek of singed hair and something fouler, the stink of rot masked by candle wax. He steadied his breathing and scanned the dimly lit room. A single candle burned near the pit in the center, its flame casting deep orange shadows.

"Who gave you life, my little friend?" Risto spoke to the candle.

Orenda stepped into the candlelight, her face illuminated by the glow.

Risto froze.

A wave of disgust knotted his stomach. This was no longer the woman he remembered; the sight of her was like staring into a nightmare, a cruel distortion of what once was. Her skin seemed stretched too tight across bone in some places, melted and sagging in others, as though fire and time had fought over her and both had won. Patches of her skin seemed melted, drawn tight around her cheekbones, with veins shadowing beneath the surface. Her limbs were thin but stretched with sinew, movements jerky and too deliberate, like a puppet tugged by invisible strings. Her eyes, once human, now glowed with an unwavering green light, sharp and unnatural.

When her gaze caught his, it pinned him like a specimen. When she smiled, her mouth stretched too wide, exposing teeth that seemed longer, darker. Her nails had blackened into claw-like points, and her tangled hair clung to her face as though recoiling from the corruption within. Power radiated from her, but it was the power of rot and ruin, not life. In the half-light, her twisted features almost resembled the very Narlocs she had birthed, as though they were not creatures she commanded but reflections of what she had become.

"Are you real, or my imagination?" Risto called out, circling the pit cautiously with his sword ready. "We left you there. I left you there."

"No," Orenda's voice boomed, lower and harsher than before, reverberating through the room. "You were right the first time. All of you left me there."

"So, you are real. How'd you do it?"

"It wasn't anything impressive, but ignorance played a part."

"You got too close. You were drawn in?" Risto said, his sword still poised.

"No. After seeing Daniel disappear through the window with your father... my curiosity got the better of me. As you followed, your jacket slipped in your hand. I grabbed hold of it, desperate not to be left behind."

Risto's face reflected his discouragement, a mistake he could have avoided, but listened.

"But cloth doesn't bleed, and that's why I didn't cross the same way you did. You all came through together, whole. I came through broken, changed. And this…" she spread her hands, her voice bitter, "this is what I became. And don't mistake me for a victim of it. I wear it proudly. It's stronger than the woman you knew."

Risto's grip on his sword tightened, his face twisting with revulsion. He could barely reconcile the monster before him with the woman he once knew.

"So now what?" Risto asked. "Why did you come back here? You're not wanted by these people anymore, and I will defend them from you."

"Defend them? They have nothing to fear from me. I will protect them."

"You can't protect them. You bring only misery and suffering. You're evil."

Hisses filled the air, startling him. He spun around, sword extended, trying to locate the source of the sound. "What was that?" he demanded.

"I don't have any idea what you're talking about. You must be hearing things."

The hissing intensified, surrounding him. It slithered through the rafters, under the floorboards, until it felt like the sound was inside his skull. Risto backed toward the door, swinging his sword wildly at the unseen threats.

"Now, my old friend, you will learn what evil really looks like," Orenda declared as the hissing morphed into a chant.

Risto screamed a battle cry, lifting his sword in defiance.

"Now!" Orenda commanded.

As the chanting peaked, Risto saw the malicious green eyes and bared teeth of his assailants. In that moment, his sword clattered to the ground, overcome by the terror of the evil unleashed around him.

9

Risto awoke to a racket that echoed the hissing of steam and the rumble of generators. His eyes remained closed, but the stark pain across his back made it evident that he was lying on a hard surface, stone, cold and unyielding. Attempting to stretch, a sharp pain shot through to his neck, causing him to wince and settle back. When he finally opened his eyes, his body felt as though it had endured a severe beating. Stretching his legs offered a brief respite, and he gingerly moved his arms, feeling the ache spread from his shoulders to his wrists. Gradually, he realized the sound he thought was machinery was actually the pounding in his head, a severe headache that throbbed.

As he became more aware of his surroundings, the harsh reality set in: he was shackled. Large metal shackles clamped around his wrists and ankles, the cold steel chafing against his skin, and he noticed his boots were missing. The chains linked to the shackles clinked against the stone floor whenever he shifted, offering a grim reminder of his captivity. He was raised off the floor, laid out on a stone slab like some offering. To his left there was nothing but a stone wall, its surface a blend of black and deep purple, smooth yet sharp. To his right, the stone extended into a ledge that ran about thirty yards before turning right into a larger area. The air smelled faintly metallic, as if rust and blood had mingled into the same dust.

The last memory Risto had before his capture at Orenda's was the eerie hissing that filled the room, now identified as the presence of something sinister she had summoned, demons, he presumed. As the pounding in his head subsided slightly, Risto replayed the hissing sounds in his mind, likening them to thousands of hands clapping in unison.

"I trust you're comfortable," Orenda's voice suddenly broke his concentration.

Startled, Risto tilted his head back and saw her looming over him, her face upside down, framed by a bleak expression and flanked by indistinct, shadowy figures that twisted in and out of visibility. Her features swam in and out of focus, as if the air around her warped under pressure.

"I'd like to be moved to the presidential suite, please," he quipped under his breath, then turned his gaze away toward the ledge.

"Ha! You still have your sense of humor, don't you?" She knelt close to his face. "Trust me, my dear, you are in the presidential suite, and I suggest you not upset the management."

hsss, hsss

"What is that I keep hearing in my head, and just now? Your new pets?"

"These are the Narlocs."

The shadowy figures beside her took more defined shapes, revealing green eyes and wide, hissing mouths. One of them extended a small hand with large claws toward Risto.

He quickly turned his face away.

"No, no, not yet. He's had enough for the moment," Orenda instructed, and the Narloc receded.

"So now what?" he asked. "What do you want?"

"All of it," she declared as the Narlocs crowded closer, their hissing vibrant with anticipation. Drool dripped close to him, almost touching.

"Just hurry up and do it," Risto urged, his patience thinning.

Orenda appeared confused. "What is this? What game is this?"

"This is no game. Do what you're going to do. Let's just get on with it. I'm tired," he said, closing his eyes.

hsss

"Hmm. Looks as if someone has lost their way, lost their faith maybe. That is, if faith is something to want," she mused, running a bony finger through his hair. Her touch left behind a faint chill, as though her skin carried nightmares.

"You're right. Maybe I have lost my faith. I'm tired of fighting you. Let's end this now."

"Oh, you won't get out of it that easily. We like to play," Orenda retorted as the Narlocs fluttered their wings.

HSSS

Risto heard movement and looked toward his feet to see a swirling black mass with pulsating green eyes approaching.

Orenda laughed. "Oh yes, we all love to play, don't we?" she exclaimed as the room filled with deafening hisses.

HSSS, HSSS

He closed his eyes, trying to block out the overwhelming sounds.

"Stop!" she commanded, and the room fell silent.

When Risto opened his eyes again, the Narlocs had vanished, but Orenda was still there, combing his hair with her hand.

"Rest easy, my friend," she cooed. "There are big things to come, and I want you to be a part of it all."

He shook his head, trying to dismiss her touch. "Go away!"

She paused momentarily, then disappeared from his sight.

"Playtime," she finally declared, signaling the Narlocs, who swiftly grabbed hold of him, their hisses resuming as they closed in.

They swarmed him, their claws raking across his chest and arms in a frenzy of hisses. One lurched close, its mouth widening unnaturally. For an instant a blinding white light flickered in its throat, then erupted into a plume of black fire. The flames licked across Risto's body, searing but not consuming, clinging like tar. The heat tore into his skin, deeper than any sunburn, almost to the bone. Smoke curled up around him as his clothes blackened and flaked away.

Risto screamed, thrashing in the chains, the stench of his own scorched flesh choking him. His vision jittered with spots of red and white, as though his very eyes were blistering. Every nerve lit with agony as the fire receded, leaving a residue of soot that clung to his body.

The Narlocs hissed in triumph, their eyes glowing brighter in the dimness. Orenda's laughter carried through the chamber, cruel and delighted, echoing over his cries.

The heat would not leave him. It pressed into him, inside and out. Darkness clawed its way into his vision. His screams dwindled to ragged gasps as the world tilted and dissolved.

10

Risto cautiously opened his eyes, taking care not to alert the nearby Narlocs. Exhaustion weighed on him, and he was coated in black soot, the residue of their black fire clinging to his skin. His body still radiated with blistering heat, every movement raw with pain. Pretending to be unconscious, he waited until the sounds of the Narlocs receded before assessing his situation.

The last thing he remembered before losing consciousness was Orenda's sinister declaration of *playtime*, followed by excruciating pain. He had always believed Narlocs to be mythical until now. The stink of them still lingered in his nose, burnt hair and sulfur. Their realness was undeniable, and their presence was unnerving. They seemed to dislike direct eye contact, becoming aggressive if stared at, something Risto had learned after receiving several scratches and warning bites.

The shackles on his wrists dug painfully into his skin, their weight immense. He carefully tested the chains for any give, fearing any noise might attract unwanted attention. The chains clinked, and a link shifted unexpectedly. Risto instantly froze, feigning unconsciousness as he felt a chilling presence hover close by. A low hiss slid across his cheek like steam from a kettle. His heart slammed against his ribs, but he forced his breathing to stay even, clinging to Drisana's memory like a lifeline. The memory of her laughter was his refuge from fear.

A sharp pain suddenly shot through his forearm. Risto clenched his teeth, enduring the Narloc's probing claw as it tried to provoke a reaction. Eventually, the pain ceased, the creature withdrawing its claw but not retreating. Risto lay still, eyes closed, grappling with despair. The Narlocs' strength seemed overwhelming, and for a moment he considered giving up.

When its presence finally faded, he cautiously opened his eyes. The room was empty except for the distant figures of Narlocs engaged in their obscure activities. He sighed and turned his head, only to catch the fleeting glimpse of green eyes still fixed on him before darkness enveloped him again.

When he next regained consciousness, his head

throbbed and his vision was clouded by swelling. The hissing of Narlocs echoed from above, hinting at their readiness to strike again. Mechanical laughter reverberated through the chamber, a sound Risto recognized all too well, Orenda's mocking tone, chilling him to the core.

Amidst the torment, Risto moaned louder, attempting to drown out the noise and her presence. His plea was desperate. "Just get it over with, for God's sake! Stop messing around and kill me already."

"Kill you? Now come on, Risto. Where's the fun in that?" Orenda's voice was cruelly playful.

"I don't want to be here anymore, Orenda. Let me go."

She paused, intrigued yet silent, then signaled for quiet. Approaching, her presence was near but unnervingly calm. "Why would you say such a thing?" she mused, echoing his earlier words in a biting imitation. "I don't want to be here anymore, Orenda. Let me go."

"Because I'm ready to leave, I guess," he said. He blinked against the swelling. His eye itched, but he couldn't scratch it, his wrists were bound tight.

"Hmm. No, I believe there might be more to this. It's not like you. You have more spirit than this. What's going on with you?"

"It's nice to know you know me so well. Maybe if you come down off the ceiling with the rest of your little babies, I'll tell you all about it. It's hard for me to say, tied up like this."

"Ha! Ceiling?" she couldn't contain her laughter. She glanced at the Narlocs. "You must have hit him too hard, he's talking crazy now."

The Narlocs erupted in a triumphant hiss. Risto winced at the noise filling the cavern. Orenda raised her hand, and the creatures fell silent. "My child. I am not on the ceiling. I'm standing only a few feet from you."

He turned his head, straining to see. The cave was dim, and with his eyes nearly swollen shut, he could make out only shifting shapes in the shadows.

"Please, old friend, let me help you," Orenda whispered as she stepped closer. She pressed one of her long, misshapen fingernails against his cheek. He flinched. The smile on her face faded as she popped her finger upward, slicing into his skin and leaving a two-inch cut.

Risto screamed and thrashed, trying to make her back away. He had endured enough. Then he noticed something different. The pain dulled as he felt the blood on his face. The blood flowed upward, sliding along his cheek, past his eye, and into his hairline. That's when it hit him, he wasn't lying down at all. He was hanging upside down.

She continued to whisper, her voice slow and deliberate, as several Narlocs paced beside her. "Can you hear me, boy? Can you?"

Risto jerked at the sound of her voice, the chain biting into his wrists as he strained. If he were standing, his pose, hands overlapped and extended forward, might resemble a man at church waiting to pass the collection plate.

"Yes, I can hear you," he said.

She studied his face, marked with bruises and burns. His eyes peered out through narrow slits. A trail of blood stained his cheek. With a strangely gentle gesture, Orenda caressed his face. "I've always cared for you, Risto. But you could never see beyond the immediate."

Risto, caught between pain and confusion, asked, "Is this the part where you let me go?"

"I don't know what game you think we're playing, but it doesn't suit you."

"There is no game."

The surrounding Narlocs hissed restlessly, their noise filling the chamber. Orenda's smile faltered. She studied him with sharp focus. "Something is different about you. You seem indifferent, almost as if you have no fight left. I hadn't expected the Narlocs to have such an effect."

Risto scoffed. "Don't be too pleased with yourself. It has nothing to do with your new pets."

The creatures hissed again, their sound swelling like a wave until Orenda silenced them again.

"Honestly, I'm just done with all this," he said, his words slurring as exhaustion overtook him. Normally he would fight back, attempt escape, or spit defiance, not hang limp as he did now.

Recognizing his fatigue, Orenda signaled to the Narlocs. "Let him down. Lay him on the floor."

A Narloc approached a large turnstile wheel, a construction of metal with protruding handles and chains. The hoist was designed to lower heavy loads, possibly into the pit within the cave. He had never seen its depths. The creature manipulated two levers. The first unlocked the chain, and the second released the wheel. Two more Narlocs joined, gripping the handles to steady the descent under Risto's weight.

As the wheel turned, Risto felt himself lowered. The squeal of iron teeth grinding against rust echoed like a scream. Dust shook loose from the cavern ceiling, drifting down in pale veils. The sensation reminded him of a night in his youth when he had drunkenly swayed in his father's barn, a vivid memory of dizziness and nausea he never repeated. Now, the slow, rhythmic ticking of the wheel was hypnotic.

tink, tink, tink

The echoes marked his gradual descent. Disoriented, he braced himself for the relief of solid ground.

The Narlocs coordinated smoothly, adjusting the wheel to keep him steady. Through swollen eyes, Risto watched the cavern rotate past in blurred fragments. He could barely make out where the edge of the cavern dropped off into the pit.

They lowered him slowly, letting his head touch first, followed by his shoulders, and then rolling him easily onto the floor until his heels rested. The cold stone beneath him felt almost comforting. The grit bit into his back, raw against his burned skin, but he welcomed it, it reminded him he was still alive.

The Narlocs unhooked him. The hoist rattled back into the shadows, echoes of the large wheel ticking in the background faded, oddly reassuring.

Orenda leaned over him, tilting her head with curiosity. "Is that better?"

"Yes," he said, his voice raw. "Are we near Hope?"

"We are far from Hope, my friend. Let's just say we're still in our own time, but perhaps somewhere in between what is…" she drew breath, "…and what is to come."

He thought of Drisana, terrified for her safety but unwilling to mention her name. He also thought of Jen. He held his fears inside, refusing to give Orenda any sort of leverage.

"In between worlds? So we're… nowhere," he said.

Orenda studied him for a long moment, her eyes narrowing as if weighing something unseen. At last she nodded. "You do seem different. The fight in you has dulled, and perhaps that is useful to me. Therefore, I've decided to release you from those shackles."

The Narlocs hissed in protest, circling restlessly. One even climbed boldly over him, making him flinch.

"Calm yourselves!" Orenda commanded. Her voice cracked through the cavern, silencing them. She leaned in closer to him. "You've suffered enough for now. But do not mistake this for mercy. You will remain here, among us, where I can watch you."

"You're going to set me free?"

"Yes. Free to walk, but not free to leave. You'll be allowed to explore, to see where you are."

Risto questioned with his eyes, listening.

"Avoid the edges if you venture outside," she said.

His expression darkened with wariness.

"You'll understand better once you see it. Who knows? Maybe you'll come to like it here. Perhaps you'll even learn to trust me again."

With a wave of her hand, she signaled to the Narlocs. "Set him free. He will remain among us. Bring him to me if he tries to escape."

As they began to unbind him, Risto felt a surge of cautious relief. Though freed from chains, the truth of his liberty was far less certain. The stone beneath him was slick with something he couldn't place, and the air itself seemed alive, pressing close as though the cave were listening. He resolved to find a way out, praying his vision would soon clear, and that he might discover some weakness in this strange place between worlds.

11

As the sun dipped below the horizon, the people of Hope congregated in the town square. Torches were being lit along the edges, their flames trembling in the growing dusk. Parents pulled children close, voices lowered to whispers that swelled together into a hum of concern.

Adriel and Daniel stood at the center of it, scanning every passing face for a sign of Risto. Their inquiries to the townsfolk yielded no sightings or news, each shake of the head adding to the unease already gathering in the square.

"Have you heard anything at all, from anyone?" Adriel pressed, his voice edged with worry.

"Nothing at all. I can't imagine where he might have gone," Daniel said.

"What about Drisana? Have you seen her?"

"No. She's missing too."

At that moment, Drisana and her friends appeared, weaving through clusters of anxious townspeople. The worry etched on Adriel's face was unmistakable. Sensing the tension, Drisana excused herself from her friends and came directly to them.

"Is there still no word from him?" she asked.

"Not a word," Adriel confirmed, his expression grave. "No one has seen him."

Daniel remained silent, but his worried eyes mirrored Drisana's fear.

"We need to start searching for him. What if something's happened? He could be hurt," she insisted.

Adriel hesitated, his tone attempting calm. "It's only been an hour. Let's not jump to conclusions just yet."

"An hour is too long already. We need to act now," she said.

Adriel placed a reassuring hand on her shoulder, trying to project steadiness for both her and himself. "I understand your worry, but let's give him a little more time. He might just need to cool off after our earlier disagreement."

Drisana searched his eyes for reassurance, but none came. The unease pressed heavier on her chest with every moment that passed. She remembered Risto's words, his halting confession of being torn through time, of living in places that were not meant for him. She wondered if his disappearance was not simply stubbornness or pride, and if it was happening again.

"Please, sit with your friends for a bit longer. I'm sure he'll show up soon," Adriel urged, gently guiding her back toward her group.

Reluctantly, she agreed, though her gaze lingered on Daniel. His forced smile faltered almost as soon as it formed. He said nothing, but in his silence she recognized the same dread beginning to settle in him.

She returned to her friends, though her thoughts were already elsewhere. Deep down, she knew something was wrong. If Risto did not return soon, she would go after him herself, no matter what Adriel said.

12

Risto could see a faint light at one end of the cave, suggesting a possible exit. As he moved, he recognized the foul stench of the Narlocs and could sense them swirling around, their movements too swift and blurred to track. They were dangerous creatures, possessing brute strength and perhaps other abilities still unknown, mind-reading, perhaps, or worse.

He followed a narrow path, the light ahead growing brighter. Sunlight filtered through the gaps in the rocks, its warmth beckoning him forward. The closer he came, the faster he moved, driven by a rising claustrophobia. When he finally emerged into the sunlight, a wave of relief washed over him. He broke into a jog, the open air fueling his stride.

Upon clearing the cave, Risto dropped to his knees,

overcome with laughter. He grabbed fistfuls of dirt, letting the soil slip through his fingers, reveling in freedom. A small, triumphant smile played across his lips as he relished his liberty.

Surveying the land, he tried to orient himself, recalling Orenda's words about being in-between worlds. Deception seemed likely, especially when he recognized a path leading toward Hope, now shrouded in a thick veil of fog.

"This is where I've been the whole time?" he asked aloud, skeptical of any caves existing nearby. He glanced back at the cave's entrance, also veiled in fog, with only a few trees visible. Moving left along the rock face, he caught sight of green eyes peering from within. For a moment he wondered if the Narlocs were bound to the cave, trapped like spirits in a bottle.

He ran a hand along the rock for balance as he stepped carefully into the fog. The mist thickened, refusing to clear. Suddenly his foot slipped. He cried out, clutching a tree to steady himself. His left leg dangled over the edge of a cliff, the roots of the tree splayed like fingers in the wind. He leaned back, dragging himself upright, then the wind stopped abruptly, freezing the moment.

Sitting now on the ground, his left leg still hanging, his right tucked beneath him, he leaned forward to peer over. As his head cleared the tree line, the wind returned, blowing his hair. He strained against the fog, glimpsing only darkness and the faint glimmer of stars far below.

The ground ended abruptly, not in rolling hills or valleys but in a sheer cut, as if the land itself had been torn away and left adrift.

"How can I be above the stars?" he said to himself.

He eased back from the cliff's edge, the wind falling still. Skirting across the rock face, he left the drop behind and passed the cave's mouth once more. From within came the hiss and stir of Narlocs, faint but undeniable, catching glimpses of green eyes staring back.

hsss, hsss

He pressed on, moving through the thick fog with care, mindful of the cliff's warning. Entering the trees, he noticed the ground felt oddly soft, the soil loose beneath his boots. The wind tousled his hair, tickling his brow. He clung to a tree and peered into the fog and the void beyond, but saw only emptiness. The realization struck him: this was no ordinary forest. The whole of it, cave, trees, and the path, rested on a vast island of land suspended in nothingness, held aloft by Orenda's magic. One wrong step and he would fall into nothing.

"What have I done? Did I cause all this madness? Will I find you again, Drisana?"

Risto realized escape was futile. He was trapped in a surreal dream, or perhaps still hanging upside down in the cave. His thoughts circled: his location, the fate of Hope, and above all, the safety of Drisana.

13

Risto trudged back to the cave, feeling defeated. He dreaded what Orenda might have planned for him, certain she would aim to destroy him, and fearing that those he loved would suffer first. Such cruelty seemed characteristic of her.

The Narlocs tracked his movements, and he advanced cautiously, unwilling to provoke them. At the back of the cave, her voice emerged from the shadows.

"Back so soon?"

He halted, startled. "Yeah, I guess I am," he said. He looked spent, a man devoid of purpose, his spirit extinguished. "There's definitely no place for me to go."

He scanned the cave, taking in the grim surroundings. Narlocs skittered around him. Orenda studied his every expression, searching for signs of the old Risto, wondering if he feigned his despondency. But she saw only a broken man before her.

"So, how'd you do it? I guess you're waiting for me to ask. And I have to admit, you've got my attention," Risto said.

"Let's just say I've found my true self these days, even the Narlocs. I found some new friends to occupy my time." she scoffed.

"Hmm. You are powerful, Orenda. I apologize for not acknowledging that before."

Her eyes narrowed suspiciously. "What are you saying? You've changed somehow. What's going on with you?"

"I don't know. Hmm. I wonder," he mused.

"Oh, I see. Okay, let's have it," she challenged, stepping closer.

"You really want to hear it? Do you?" His frustration peaked. He wiped the sweat from his brow and pushed his hair back in one sharp motion, his patience fraying. "When we were kids, teenagers at the park that night, we left because we were afraid. We thought we were running for our lives, trying to escape. Do you recall that?"

Orenda listened silently, lips pressed tight.

"That's what people do when they're afraid of something. They run. What did you expect? Then we end up back in Hope, and everyone's asking questions like we're some kind of lost heroes returning from battle. I didn't like any of it. I just wanted some peace and quiet, and maybe, just maybe, a little normality."

Her gaze held steady as he paced, her expression unreadable.

"Then *you* show back up," he said, pointing at her accusingly. "Of course you're pissed off, I get that. Then I'm taken prisoner, and here you are again, trying to prove how powerful you are. I'm apparently trapped on some sort of floating forest-cave-cloud, wondering what to do next, and yet all I can think of is to jump off the son of a bitch."

His voice echoed against the stone, ragged and raw. He turned away, pacing, his boots grinding against the rock. Orenda's lips curved faintly, but her eyes remained hard.

"So dramatic. You always had a way with words, Risto. But here you are, still alive, still in my world. Don't mistake that for freedom."

He laughed bitterly. "Freedom? You've built a cage in the sky and expect me to bow to you for the privilege of breathing in it."

"Perhaps. Or perhaps you're exactly where you belong, dangling between hope and despair, unable to choose either. That's who you are."

His hands clenched at his sides. "No. That's who you made me."

For a moment, silence stretched between them, broken only by the restless hiss of the Narlocs shifting in the shadows.

"Careful," she whispered. "That edge you cling to, the one between defiance and surrender, it will decide your fate."

He met her gaze with a tight jaw. "Then maybe it's time someone pushed back."

Her eyes glistened, sharp as glass. "Try."

* * *

Drisana frantically searched the crowd, her desperation evident as she cried, "Have you seen him? Have you seen him?" She barely paused to hear the replies as she moved from one group to another. Her friends watched, stricken by the anguish in her eyes.

The townspeople clustered in groups, whispering uneasily. It was unlike Risto to vanish without a trace; his whereabouts were usually known to those closest to him.

The wind began to rise, shifting from gentle gusts to violent squalls that whipped leaves and debris through the air. Children shielded their faces or clung to their mothers. Parents scooped them up, holding them close against the biting wind. Trees bent dramatically, bowing under its weight.

"What is this?" Daniel shouted over the roar.

"I've never seen anything like it!" Adriel said, squinting against the flying debris.

The sky above darkened ominously. Still, Drisana pressed on, her voice hoarse. "Have you seen Risto?" she called again and again, but heads only shook. Panic grew as the storm intensified.

"Adriel!" she screamed, retracing her steps toward where she had last seen him and Daniel.

The two men stood in the square, watching the townsfolk scatter, clutching their children, dodging loose animals that had broken free in fright.

"There she is!" Adriel shouted.

Daniel ran to meet her, his arm around her shoulders as they hurried back to Adriel.

Then the hissing began.

A sharp, unnatural sound cut through the gale, rising above the storm. Drisana and Daniel froze, hearts pounding. Adriel's eyes widened. The hiss came again, louder, morphing into a shriek that tore through the darkening sky.

"Look!" Adriel pointed upward.

Shadows churned in the clouds, multiplying, twisting. White clouds blackened, blotting out the sun. Lightning flickered, and thunder rumbled deep. Drisana's stomach turned. This was Orenda's doing. She felt it in her bones.

The storm thickened. The three huddled together. Drisana buried her face in Daniel's chest, clutching him desperately.

"We need to get out of here!" Daniel yelled.

"Yes!" Drisana cried.

Adriel gripped their arms. "Wait! What is that?"

Bolts of lightning descended slowly from the clouds, weaving together in intricate patterns. A web of light spread across the heavens, forming a dome that enclosed them, a lattice work of living fire. The thunder roared, but the lattice held, glowing with eerie stillness. Then, evenly, the dome's sides began to descend.

Drisana clutched Daniel's shirt so tightly her nails dug into him. He winced, but she didn't let go. Their eyes locked upward as another shriek cut through the air. She pressed her face to Daniel's chest, bracing against the silence that followed.

There was no wind, no thunder, and no shrieking.

"Drisana," Daniel's voice broke the silence.

She lifted her head. Adriel and Daniel were staring upward, still in disbelief. She followed their gaze. Points of green light glimmered in the clouds.

A blinding flash erupted, thunder cracking in its wake. The web-dome slammed into the earth with crushing force. The impact threw them from their feet, and the square erupted in chaos. Tremors rippled through the ground as the dome rose and struck again, and again, each blow like a colossal hammer cutting deeper into the soil.

Drisana, Daniel, and Adriel fought to stay upright as the ground quaked, but the dome held. Screams rang out. People scrambled, clutching their children, clinging to one another in terror. Then the tremors ceased. The air fell unnervingly still.

"We need to move," Drisana urged, her voice shaking.

"Where?" Adriel said. "We're surrounded."

"We have to try!" she insisted.

A strange buzzing rose in the air, rattling through their chests.

"What is that?" Drisana whispered.

The hum poured from the dome, vibrating through the ground.

"Look, Mom! Birds!" a child cried, pointing upward. A woman screamed, dragging her child away.

Adriel turned. Large, dark shapes wheeled along the outside of the dome. They were too fast to be birds, their wings ragged, their cries sharp enough to cut through the air. Their numbers swelled until the sky seemed full of them, circling like vultures over prey.

"Are those birds… or bats?" Daniel said.

Drisana's stomach knotted. The shapes pressed close to the dome but never entered, their claws raking sparks against the lightning lattice. Each shriek echoed, and still they circled, waiting.

"What are they? What do they want?" Daniel asked.

"I don't know," Adriel said.

Drisana still clung to Daniel, her heart racing as the creatures flew overhead.

Then, silence. The buzzing was gone.

Risto. Her mind screamed for him. *Where are you? I need you.*

She looked up. "Do you see that?"

"What?" Daniel asked.

"The sky… it's changing," she said.

Adriel squinted, trying to see what she did. "I don't see. Wait! We're moving. The ground, it's lifting!"

Daniel's face went pale. "How?"

Drisana pulled free of Daniel's grip and pointed. "Don't you see? The dome isn't moving. We are."

Fog thickened around them, spreading into the forest as the ground lurched upward.

"We're floating," Daniel gasped.

The lattice held firm above them, glowing. As Hope rose higher, it pierced through the clouds, and sunlight spilled across the town. But as awe turned to fear, the truth was evident. Not only was it floating, but the land itself was shrinking, drawing inward.

"That road used to run all the way to the oak," a man cried, pointing to the empty boundary. Where a tree had stood, only raw earth marked its absence. Fences ended short. Gardens narrowed. Homes leaned, as if the soil beneath them slouched toward the center. News spread that the world was getting smaller.

Above them the dome crackled and adjusted, the lightning arcs crawling inward to match the shrinking ground. No one could leave. The circle was collapsing with steady pressure, relentless as fire spreading through dry brush.

The change could no longer be denied. And when night fell, the dread only deepened. Families huddled together in the dark, too frightened to sleep, or taking shifts to keep watch. Some of the children finally drifted off, but even in dreams their faces twitched with unease, as though they could feel the land changing beneath them.

Hope was shrinking.

14

Phineas hurled a rock with all his strength, watching as it struck a tree and ricocheted unpredictably. He nodded in satisfaction, a triumphant snarl curling across his lips. He was near the edge of the forest, far from town, where he often found himself stirring up mischief. At ten years old, Phineas was a scruffy boy with a wiry frame and the tenacity to match any older child in Hope, perhaps even more. He relished his independence, insisting on making his own choices. The townsfolk called him tough as nails.

A distinctive birthmark covered his right eye, earning him the nickname Patch, which he wore proudly. Only his mother and one other person were allowed to call him by his real name, Phineas. Anyone else who tried risked his wrath. That other person was Risto. Patch allowed Risto to use his true name and even welcomed it. There was something soothing about hearing it from him.

Despite the twenty year age gap, Patch and Risto shared a bond. Patch looked up to him as a father figure, something his life sorely lacked, and Risto treated him with the respect of an equal. Patch knew that if he ever needed help, Risto would be there.

As Patch wandered through the forest, he gathered rocks and hurled them at anything in sight. Birds made the most challenging targets, and he was thrilled at the rare chance of hitting one in mid-flight. He also searched for large branches to serve as a walking staff or a mock weapon. Talking to himself as he walked, he imagined himself a warrior, sometimes a sorcerer, bracing for the next enemy to cross his path.

His destination was Devil's Edge, a cliff with a sheer drop of twelve to fifteen feet that ended in a sloped embankment, perfect for rock-hurling and staging battles in his imagination.

Risto was already there, hidden behind a boulder, waiting. They often arranged these meetings, carving out time for just the two of them.

"Take that!" Patch shouted, swinging a dead branch at an imaginary foe. "Back where you came from!" The branch whooshed as it cut the air. "Take the rest of your men in hiding with you, or our dragons will find them, and you as well!"

Risto smiled as he listened, appreciating the boy's passion. He had once promised to teach Patch sword fighting, admiring his eagerness and grit.

Stepping from behind the boulder, Risto drew his sword and shouted, "Never surrender!"

Patch whirled, startled but ready, swinging his branch to deflect the strike. "Of course you'd sneak up from behind, you coward!"

Risto grinned. "You know me all too well."

"And that, my friend, will be your downfall."

Dropping to one knee, Risto held his sword upright. "It is a great honor to be your friend. One day, you *will* be a fierce warrior."

Patch extended his hand. "Rise, my friend. And thank you for your guidance and training."

Risto stood, and they both burst into laughter.

"It's good to see you, kid," Risto said.

"You too!" Patch replied, hugging him.

"You swing one mean piece of deadwood."

"What, this old thing?" Patch waved the branch before tossing it aside. "I'm a better shot with rocks."

"Oh really?" Risto lifted the branch, balancing it on his fingers. "On the count of three," he said, preparing to throw it into the air.

Patch quickly selected a stone, then grabbed a second for good measure.

"One... two..." Risto flung the branch skyward before finishing the count.

Caught off guard, Patch focused quickly, gauging its flight. He adjusted his stance, drew back, and hurled the rock with surprising force.

Risto's face lit with astonishment as the stone struck the branch with a solid thud.

"Last I checked, three came after two," Patch said, scratching his head.

"Just keeping you sharp, kid. Good shot." Risto winked. "You really are good at that. It's amazing, actually. You've got a gift. You could use those stones as weapons if you had to."

Patch eyed the branch where it landed. "Yeah. I like doing it. Feels natural."

Risto rested a hand on his shoulder. "Then never forget how it feels. The world's going to test you someday."

15

Risto opened his eyes. He was back on the slab, hands and feet bound. It was business as usual. His right shoulder ached from having lain on it too long. At least Orenda had allowed the chains to be long enough for him to turn over while he slept, but the hard surface was merciless.

He missed Patch. The memory of the boy reminded him how much he liked him, good kid, good heart. *If only he were here,* he thought. Patch would not hesitate to fight, but that also scared him. Patch never wanted to see anyone suffer. He would fight with his heart, but sometimes that wasn't enough. Sometimes you had to fight dirty. If Patch got involved, the Narlocs might catch him off guard, and there were just too many of them.

He rolled onto his back and stared up at the rocks overhead, while Drisana's face came to him. *How had it come to this?* he thought. He felt defeated—beaten. Orenda had walked back into his life, taking a turn he never expected. He had trusted her, looked up to her when he was younger. She had shown him the secrets of the necklace, the amulet. She was smart, and maybe she had been planning this moment all along, or maybe it had simply gone to hell. Either way, here he lay, stripped of his belongings, bound, unsure what would come next.

* * *

Night fell over Hope. The townspeople lingered outside, afraid, uncertain, trying to keep close. Families huddled together, whispering in low voices. Those with children worked to maintain a veneer of normalcy, food, water, small comforts. Out beyond the glow of their fires, a figure moved through the fog, quiet and sure. Patch had returned. He was fifteen now, older but still carrying the same fierce spark Risto remembered from his youth.

"Patch, where have you been?" Thea asked.

"I've been exploring. Looking for clues. Maybe figure out what's going on." He sat beside his mother under a small tree, sword at his hip. "Do you have anything to eat?"

"Of course." Thea opened a blanket at her side and produced bread and strips of beef, tough like jerky. "Here.

You need your strength."

"Thank you, Mother." Patch devoured it quickly.

She handed him a small container of water. "Easy. Slow down. You'll choke."

Patch scooped it into his mouth so fast it ran down both sides of his face.

"So, where have you been? Have you discovered anything?"

"I went as far as the old hill to the east and the petrified woods in the west," he said, but the rhythm of his chewing slowed. He looked at his mother with sorrow in his eyes.

"What's wrong? What did you see?" she asked.

"I never made it to either place. It's true, the landscape is shrinking."

Thea looked away, afraid.

"Normally, it would take almost half a day to reach either point, but I made the journey to both in a couple of hours. The dome stops at the edge, but it *is* getting closer."

"You need to be careful, Patch. They say those creatures, the ones we saw flying, are what lifted us, what keeps us here. I don't know what they are."

"No one does," he said.

Thea studied her son. She knew he would make a fine warrior someday, brave and determined. Risto had done him good, taught him to fight, taught him strength. She had always been thankful for that.

"Well, we may not know, but something tells me they're pure evil. Maybe the devil himself, or his minions," she said.

"Little devils?" Patch laughed, crumbs falling from his lips.

"Don't mock me." She pinched his arm lightly. "And chew your food."

"Ow! Now who's being evil?"

She gave him a look of disapproval. He swallowed, grinned, and both burst out laughing.

"It's hard to be angry with you," she admitted. "I love you too much. I just want you safe."

Patch drank again, then set the container down. "I know you worry, but I'm okay. You have to believe me. I'm being careful. Staying out of sight."

"I know you are. I do believe you. But promise me you won't do anything reckless. Don't try to be a hero. This is real."

"Well, someone has to be."

"You're right. Someone does. I just don't know why it has to be you." She hesitated, her voice low. "But something tells me you're tied to this place in a way the rest of us aren't. Maybe that's why it has to be you."

Patch looked at her, seeing her concern. "Oh, Mother." He wrapped his arms around her. "You've nothing to worry about. This will work itself out. You'll see."

She held him tightly, tears rising. "I know you'll do your best. Just please, be careful."

"I will."

She kissed his forehead. "Take some food with you, then come back and tell me what those little devils are up to."

"Deal!" Patch grinned. He gathered his things and slipped into the forest.

He moved quickly through the trees. The fog thickened until he could see only a few feet ahead. The gnarled trunks seemed alive, bending in the mist, aware of him. He could not shake the feeling of being watched. He stopped, glancing over his shoulder. A soft rustle came from above. He looked up.

From the fog a figure descended, cloaked in fire. White wings spread wide, but they did not simply gleam— they burned, every feather rimmed in flame, alive and shifting as if the air itself were kindling. The light was not steady; it flickered and roared, like a living blaze wrapped around a human form. Heat shimmered from the being's body, flames licking along its arms and shoulders as though it were both flesh and fire, spirit and storm. The ground quivered beneath its landing, the air bending with the weight of its presence.

Patch drew his sword, bracing for one of those shadow creatures. But as the figure neared, he saw the fire was not destruction, but glory. Its face was kind, red and yellow danced in its eyes steady. It was neither man nor woman, androgynous, but beautiful all the same.

"You must be Patch," the being said, voice soft as a breeze.

Patch stood frozen. "Are you... an angel?"

The figure smiled. "Of sorts. I am Lucian. I am here to aid you and Risto. Darkness has taken hold of Hope, but together we can fight it." His voice boomed with power, carrying the weight of something divine.

Resolve surged in Patch's chest. "Risto! Do you know where he is?"

Lucian nodded. "He is in Orenda's grasp. His spirit is strong, but he doesn't realize that yet. He seems to have lost faith in himself. With your help, we can free him and restore balance."

Patch's eyes burned with determination. "What do we need to do? Where did you come from? How is this even possible?"

Lucian extended a hand, light radiating from his touch. "When darkness gathers, we appear. Not before, not after. Now is the time."

Patch stared in awe as the warmth washed through him.

Lucian's gaze held steady. "We could sweep the darkness away ourselves, but then nothing would change. Your people would remain powerless, waiting for others to save them. That is why you must walk with us. You are of Hope. Only by standing with us will your people find their strength again, and through that strength, both the land and its spirit can be restored."

Patch swallowed hard, the weight of those words sinking in. For the first time, he felt as if the future of Hope rested not on angels or warriors of legend, but on people like him.

"Now we must gather allies. There are others like me, waiting. Together, we will defeat Orenda and her Narlocs."

"Narlocs?" Patch asked.

"Living shadows of evil, direct reflections of Orenda, consuming all in their path."

Lucian pulled Patch in closer. "Come, little one. I will need your help."

Patch held on tight. Lucian lifted his gaze skyward, wings beating. Together they rose, trailing a streak of iridescent light until they vanished.

They crossed enchanted forests, shimmering lakes, and towering mountains, seeking others. Each angel was unique, wielding their own gifts. Aurelius could create blinding light to disorient foes. Zephyr controlled the wind, carrying messages and speeding their flight. Together they grew into a formidable band, each devoted to saving Hope.

As they traveled, Patch listened, learning of the angels' ancient struggle against darkness. With every step, his sense of purpose deepened. For the first time, he understood the true weight of courage. He understood the meaning of sacrifice.

16

Risto lay in chains. Though weakened, he refused to break. He thought of Drisana, of Patch, of the people of Hope, and their memory gave him strength. He still felt lost, as he had for so long. Yet deep within, a faint flutter stirred, a fire that whispered: *don't give up.*

Orenda stood over him, gloating. "You are alone, Risto. No one can save you now."

He didn't respond. He closed his eyes, holding fast to the ember within, willing it to grow. *Bring light into this darkness,* he thought, a silent plea. A breeze stirred the cave dust, and he opened his eyes, sensing a strange energy in the air.

Orenda quickly looked to the entrance of the cave, feeling the same thing. "Go," she snapped to one of the Narlocs. "Something's not right. Look outside."

The creature darted off.

At the cave's entrance, the Narloc crawled upward, clinging to stone, scanning the forest. The night was deep, the hour well past midnight, and the moon hung low. The creature spotted the silhouette of a boy with moonlight behind him and sword in hand. The Narloc smelled his fear and descended.

Patch saw its eyes. His throat tightened, and he swallowed hard.

"Never fear, little one. We are with you. Stand strong." The words rang inside his head—Lucian's voice.

Patch raised his sword, though his arms trembled. Sweat stung his eye. He wiped it, gripping the hilt tighter.

The Narloc quickened its pace, hungry for fear.

"Step forward," Lucian instructed. The command echoed again.

Patch blinked, adjusted his stance, and obeyed, left foot steady, right sliding forward, blade raised in defiance.

The Narloc leapt, mouth open, claws extended. But before it could strike, wings of light spread behind the boy. A wall of radiance stopped the beast mid-air. It dropped, writhed, and turned to dust, carried away in the wind.

Patch lowered his sword, stunned. Behind him stood Lucian, arm outstretched and white wings extended in an orange glow, ever-burning.

"Thank you," Patch said.

"Do not be afraid," Lucian told him. "Fight with all your might. You are under our protection."

Patch looked at his arms. They glowed faintly, dusted with gold. "Whoa. I have a shield on my body."

Lucian nodded, then turned back to the cave, his face hardening. "On my command," he said to the host that flanked him.

"What's taking so long?" Orenda shouted.

Light burst into the cave. Shadows and radiance collided. Narlocs shrieked as they charged headlong into beams of fire, bursting into dust. Wings flashed across the cavern, bursts of energy flaring, blinding and beautiful. The host surged forward in a flood, cutting through the dark. Patch ran at their side, his sword flashing as the first Narlocs fell beneath fire and steel.

From where he lay, Risto strained to see. The din of battle shook the stone.

Orenda shouted, summoning her creatures, but the host pressed in, radiant light driving her back step by step. Then the angels spoke, their voices like rolling thunder, words reverberating through the stone, shaking the cavern walls.

She screamed, calling up her powers, but they faltered against the invading brilliance. Her Narlocs scattered, unable to withstand the assault. Through the swirling dust, she locked eyes with Lucian, seeing all his might, stature, and presence. His form blazed.

"It can't be," she demanded, her voice breaking, and took a step back, almost cowering. "Who are you?"

"I am fire," he answered simply. His voice rolled like heat itself, both comforting and deadly. Flames danced along his hand, alive with red, orange, and yellow.

Orenda faltered. Her own power dimmed against his.

Lucian's expression softened, though his resolve did not. He thrust his hand forward, and fire engulfed her, not burning, but binding. Heat wrapped tight around her arms, forcing her hands together before her. The radiant blaze held fast, a living tether of flame. Gasping, she fell to the ground, subdued yet unharmed.

* * *

The battle raged across Hope. Angels clashed with the Narlocs, fire and thunder rippled through the sky.

In the town square, Adriel, Drisana, and Daniel clung to one another as the dome convulsed. The lattice of lightning cracked under the strain, opening tears that let Narlocs pour in like carrion birds. Their shrieks split the air. One seized a screaming woman, hurling her over the ledge before a fire angel cut it from the sky. Another plowed into a knot of townsfolk, claws slashing, until an angel dropped like a comet, wings blazing, scattering it like ash.

Drisana screamed as the ground shook beneath them. A Narloc landed hard, forcing Daniel to shove her aside. He reached for a nearby pickaxe someone had been using for defense and swung. It struck the Narloc, but Daniel was slashed across his forearm before he could strike again, forcing him to drop the weapon. The Narloc's jaws opened wide for him, stepping closer, then lunged. Before it struck, fire swept in, an angel's blade flashing, the creature split apart in a burst of sparks and smoke. The heat was so close it scorched Daniel's skin, but the angel never faltered, moving like a living flame through the chaos.

After seeing Daniel fight the Narloc, some of the townspeople pulled together with whatever they could find, and began to fight back, others fled. Narlocs gave chase, dragging more to the edge, dropping them over before angelic wings swept through, intercepting, saving who could be saved. But not all were spared. Screams rose as the battle raged.

Above them the dome groaned, fractures streaking across its surface. Lightning cascaded wildly, arcs snapped close to the earth. Adriel raised his arm to shield his eyes, his voice breaking. "It's breaking! It's coming down!" he yelled, pointing.

The lattice broke. With a deafening crack, it shattered

outward, shards of lightning flung into the void like broken spears. The false dome dissolved, its brilliance collapsed in on itself. Hope lurched, the ground tilted, then steadied as if it were seized by vast unseen hands. Slowly, the city began to descend, guided through smoke and floating embers. The angels soared above it like blazing sentinels. Cries rose from the townspeople, fear and awe colliding, as their home was carried back toward the earth.

"Look!" Drisana cried, pointing skyward as the host gathered above them, wings beating in rhythm. Together they sang, a hymn older than the earth itself, and their voices guided the city's descent. Hope lowered, trembling, steadied by fire and light, until the land itself caught it once more.

The people collapsed where they stood, gasping, sobbing, clinging to the earth. Ash, smoke, and sparks drifted down through the silence where fire had once torn the sky, but the city was no longer adrift. Hope had returned.

* * *

At Risto's side, a shape emerged through the brilliance. Another of the host, face stern, eyes burning like white coals, reached for his chains. They began to hum. At first only a tingle against his skin, then a rising pulse. Energy coursed through him as the links quivered, splintered, and fell away.

He staggered to his feet, coughing, his breath ragged. A hand touched his shoulder, guiding him away. He turned, glimpsing golden wings, then the figure vanished into the chaos.

Trusting the unseen presence, Risto staggered toward the entrance. From there, he saw Patch, no longer the boy he remembered, but a warrior haloed in light, sword flashing, cutting Narlocs down one by one. Dust burst around him with each strike.

Pride swelled in Risto's chest, tempered by confusion. "How is this possible?"

The cave fell still.

"Go," a voice urged in his head. "Go to safety at the edge."

He obeyed, stumbling into the night, but as he neared the mouth of the cave, a Narloc broke free of the fray, wings beating hard against the smoke. It lunged, seized Risto by his shoulders, cutting into him. Risto let out a cry, but was carried away in its claws, and hauled into the open air.

The beast soared outward, dragging Risto high over the cliff. Then, with a sudden shriek, it released him, casting him into the void and banking away into the night.

The wind roared past Risto, nothing but blackness and

stars. In his mind, he saw Orenda's face twisted in a triumphant smile, her eyes gleaming with malice.

"Risto!" Patch screamed.

In a blaze of motion, Lucian dove, wings shimmering with fire. He caught Risto mid-fall, the heat of his grasp burning through the cold rush of the void. With each powerful stroke, Lucian slowed their descent, carrying him down past the cliff's edge. The ground rose beneath them, solid and sure.

Risto felt the air change, the shimmer of unreality peeling away. The strange, twisted realm Orenda had created began to collapse, its false light dimming as the true world returned. The ground beneath them steadied. The pain and scars that had gripped his body were gone, lifted, healed by fire not meant to wound but to restore.

Then, above them, wings of flame split the darkness. Adriel, Drisana, Daniel, and the townspeople lifted their eyes, every face turned skyward. Awe rippled through the crowd, and prayers were whispered as mothers clutched children. The whole of Hope bore witness as the angels carried Risto home.

Risto looked like a child in Lucian's arms. Lucian carefully set him down, helping him get a foothold.

"My pain seems to have gone or healed, maybe both. I feel very warm, comforted," Risto said, dazed by the glow of Lucian's hands.

Lucian's eyes burned like coals, alive with flame.

"Who... who are you?" Risto asked.

"I am Lucian. I am here to protect you. Your courage drew us here."

Before Risto could speak again, two more of the host descended, carrying Patch, and Orenda, bound.

"Risto! Are you okay?" Patch cried, rushing to him.

"I'm fine. Thanks to him," Risto said, nodding to Lucian, who returned the reaction. Then Risto's eyes moved to Orenda. "Why? Why all this?"

Her voice hissed with defiance. "The power of Hope belongs to me."

Lucian's voice cut steady and firm. "Hope was meant as a beacon, not a weapon. It survives only when its people stand together. Divided, you fall. United, you are stronger than any darkness."

Orenda spat. "You fools. You've blinded yourselves. I will destroy Hope."

Lucian's gaze locked on Orenda. "Your time is over. This ends now."

Still bound in fire, she writhed, her lips curling into something bitter. Her fingers worked against one another, twisting a black-stoned ring. Quietly, almost beneath the clash of voices, she began to whisper an incantation.

The host stood together, speaking in tones almost too beautiful to endure. The people of Hope pressed closer, relief surging through the crowd, unaware of the danger building at its center. A faint gray light now edged the horizon, the first whisper of dawn pushing back the night.

Then smoke erupted and shadows boiled from Orenda's form, swallowing the fire that bound her, floating away in the wind. Her body warped as she rose, more shadow than flesh, eyes burning with malice. Then, in a rush, she vanished. The plume of smoke reappeared an instant later behind Drisana. The crowd gasped as a dagger of shadow kissed the girl's throat.

"Stay back!" Orenda snarled, dragging Drisana toward the trees. "One step closer, and she dies. Leave me, all of you. Do it, or watch her fall."

Risto lunged, fury breaking from him, but Lucian raised a hand, holding him fast. Lucian leaned close, his voice barely a whisper. "See."

Risto froze, his eyes straining through the dark. And then, he did just that—he *did* see. He backed up a step and waited.

Orenda tightened her grip on Drisana, turning her head just enough to sneer at the crowd.

In that moment, Patch struck. His blade pierced into her side, letting out black smoke, evil. She let out a horrific cry, then twisted to face him, eyes wide in shock. For the first time, her voice failed her. She staggered back, clutching the hilt with Patch. For an instant she tried to summon shadow, but nothing came. Drisana dropped from Orenda's grasp and ran to Risto. They met in an embrace filled with tears and relief.

Patch looked into Orenda's eyes. "Hope was never yours to take."

She drew a short breath, anticipating, and Patch thrust the sword deeper into her. "It's over," he whispered.

The strength drained from Orenda's limbs. The dagger fell from her hand, and her feet lost their way, collapsing underneath her. She fell and dissipated into dust, her cry fading into silence as the wind scattered what remained.

For a long breath, no one moved. Then the host stepped forward, wings stretching wide as if to seal the night itself. They raised their hands, and flames stood upward, scouring the air. The ground trembled. Every lingering trace of darkness shuddered and unraveled, fleeing into the trees and burning away.

Their voices rose together, like a hymn older than the earth. It carried such beauty that the people wept, not from sorrow but from awe. Light poured from them, arcing across the city of Hope, stitching it whole again. Wounds closed, walls steadied, and hearts within the crowd swelled with a strength that was not their own. One by one, the host folded their wings. The fire dimmed, but a warmth remained, settling over the people like a mantle. Relief crashed through the square in waves, gasps, sobs, cheers, the release of a city held too long in fear.

Hope was saved.

Risto stood beside Patch, his face still damp with tears. "Do you know who they were?"

Patch looked up, eyes reflecting the glow that lingered in the clouds. "I met Lucian. He and the others came to help us. He didn't tell me everything, but he said they come only when darkness gathers, never before, never after. They fight with us, not above us. They're guardians."

Risto nodded, awe filling him.

Hope had been tested, broken, nearly lost. Whatever they were, whatever had carried Hope through the storm, it still stood, alive in the hearts of its people, bound in light and courage.

The two of them stepped forward together. Side by side, they lifted their eyes over the people of Hope, the rising sun spilling gold across their faces. Patch planted his sword in the earth, while Risto's hand rested on the hilt with him. Both stood silent as watchmen of a city reborn.

Risto believed now that true hope had never left them. And never would.

About The Author

Matthew Gene lives in Ft. Worth, TX with his wife, Karen Murray Odom, author of "Mr. Owl and the Little Boy", and their dog Diesel.

www.ingramcontent.com/pod-product-compliance
Lightning Source LLC
Chambersburg PA
CBHW020826260626
47169CB00003B/844